Merry Christmas

With lots of love,

Nana & Papa - Dec 25, 2001

D0959919

A Prairie as Wide as the Sea

The Immigrant Diary of Ivy Weatherall

BY SARAH ELLIS

London, England
1926

May 1, 1926

107 Halley Road, Forest Gate, London, England

My name is Ivy Doris Weatherall. I am eleven years old. This is the first diary I have ever had. Auntie Lou gave it to me because she said that I was starting the greatest adventure of my life and I should record it. The greatest adventure is that we are emigrating to Canada. Auntie Lou also gave me a fountain pen. I am going to use my best penmanship and I am going to write every day. She also gave me a book called *Lost in the Backwoods,* which is a Canadian story. Auntie Lou is the kindest relative. I wish she were coming to Canada too.

We leave tomorrow. All our things are packed into trunks and hampers. We are camping in our house. Tonight all the relatives are coming to say goodbye. I can't wait until tomorrow. I wish I could snap my fingers and make it be now. I wish I were a conjurer. I would pull tomorrow out of a hat.

Mother just came and said I should go down to the pub and fetch Dad. He's saying goodbye to his mates. I told her I was busy recording the greatest adventure of my life and why couldn't William go. She said I was being cheeky and I had five minutes and then she wanted to see the back of me going out the door.

So now I am just going to write some facts. We are Mother, Dad, William (14), me, and the twins, Harry and Gladys (6). We are emigrating to Milorie, Saskatchewan, where our Uncle Alf has a ranch. A ranch is like a farm with horses and cows, but much grander.

Secret promise: When I grow up I'm not going to forget what it was like being a child, like almost all grown-ups seem to.

One sad thing about emigrating is that we have to leave Chivers behind. Cats aren't allowed to emigrate. I gave him to Ethel next door.

May 2

On board the Ausonia, *4 o'clock*

We're off. A man standing near me pointed out the Scilly Isles and said it was the last we would see of the old country. I watched them until they disappeared.

Goodbye, England. Goodbye, Auntie Lou. Goodbye, Chivers.

I'm sitting on the deck of our ship. There is a sheltered place around the end of one of the lifeboats. It is a fine day. Dad says that is a good omen.

More happened today than happens in a month of ordinary life. Early this morning Mother and I and the twins took the train to Southampton. Dad and William went in a lorry — Dad says that Canadians call it a truck — with our things. I wanted to go in the lorry too. But Mother said no. Why do boys get to do more things? But we did get Cadbury chocolate for the train.

At the dock there were so many people. People crowded on the pier, people coming out of carriages. Thousands of bags and trunks. And everybody was shouting questions. "Is that our ship?" "Where's Frank?" "What are we stopping for?" "Who's got the luggage?" It was like the Tower of Babel. I kept hold of a twin with either hand.

We had to walk by a medical inspector, a doctor in a gold braided uniform. He looked very grand and stern. He peered at the twins and he looked into Dad's eyes. I suddenly got frightened. What if he looked at me and thought I was sickly? Sometimes I get wheezy in the winter. What if the whole family were turned back? In a flash I saw us all standing on the dock crying as the ship pulled away. So I tried to walk with good posture and look sturdy. He hardly glanced at me.

Mother says I'm like one of the sillies in the story, rushing to meet trouble halfway. But I can't help it. Tragic stories just pop into my head.

When the ship pulled away all the people waved and shouted. We didn't have any family on the dock but we waved anyway. Mother got weepy.

Our cabin is very cunning with everything so neat and small. Soon we will all go to the dining room. Dad just came to find me. He was singing "Life on the Ocean Wave."

Later

Dinner was lovely. Ice cream for sweet. Even more delicious than the ices at home. We sat at a table with a family from Bristol. They are going to Manitoba. The father is a milkman. He and Dad talked about the general strike and how England is hopeless for the working man and all the usual dull adult things. They were talking as though we were poor. It made me angry. We're not. Poor is like the little match girl, ragged and freezing. Just because we're not toffs riding around in motor cars doesn't mean we're poor. When the rent collector came on Fridays we could nearly always pay.

I like having a diary. You can say things you're not allowed to say out loud.

The Bristol family has a boy my age. His name is Lloyd and he has ginger hair and freckles. He can wiggle his ears. He made the twins laugh so much that Gladys fell off her chair.

May 3

I love sleeping in our cabin. I was too excited to go to sleep right away so I just lay there and listened to everybody breathing. I had a dream about riding a horse, except it was riding across the ocean.

After breakfast Lloyd and William and I went exploring. Lloyd is very jolly. We came to a sign that said "Third Class Passengers Not Allowed Beyond This Point" and William was all for turning back. (William is inclined to be too well behaved.) But Lloyd put on a funny foreign accent and said, "I don't read the English, do you?" So of course we said no. We carried on and found the first-class dining room. It is like Buckingham Palace, with silver, and chandeliers with diamonds. We peeked in the windows but then one of the officers found us and made us go back to third class. He was nice, though. I suppose we would be in trouble if Mother found out but she didn't.

I have started reading *Lost in the Backwoods*. It is about pioneer families in Canada. There are three children, Catharine, her brother Hector and her cousin Louis. Catharine is twelve.

Tomorrow is lifeboat drill.

May 4

At lifeboat drill you don't get to go in the lifeboats. Gladys was so disappointed she cried. The alarm sounded and we put on our life jackets and went to our muster station. (I thought it was mustard station but when I asked William what mustard had to do with it he told me it was muster. William never taunts me if I get something wrong.) There was a little talk by one of the officers. But that was it.

Gladys cheered up when she found it was the infant's tea today. There are so many treats on this ship. She and Harry brought back a little printed programme. They had Jack Horner tarts, Mermaid cake, Mother Hubbard mixed biscuits and Father Neptune ice cream.

I am sitting next to Dad on a deck chair. He just said wasn't this the life of Riley and all we had to do was eat, sleep and be agreeable. Who was Riley? Lloyd said that one of the ship's crew told him that there is weather coming up.

Catharine, Hector and Louis just got lost in the forest. They are being very brave and resourceful. When I'm in Canada I'm going to be resourceful. There wasn't that much chance to be resourceful on Halley Road. Lloyd and I are going to sneak into first class again after dinner.

May 7

When I said I was going to write in this diary every day I didn't know about sea sickness. Sea sickness is the worst thing in the world. It is worse than measles, mumps and chicken pox. Tuesday night a storm started and the ship started pitching up and down. At first it was exciting and Harry kept wanting to go to the muster station. But then I started to feel very green. Then I lost my dinner. Then Dad got sick. Then Gladys. Then Mother. Then William. We just kept passing round the basin. Only Harry wasn't sick. The worst thing is that it just goes on and on. The ship goes up and there is a horrible little pause and then it goes down and a bit sideways. You think you would be happy to die. Harry kept poking his head in the door and saying cheerfully, "Still puking?" Mother said he was unfeeling and vulgar.

I was sick for a day and then I had soda crackers and then I slept for a day. Now I'm dandy.

There is a kind chaplain on board. He came and took Harry to meals and minded him whilst we were all in bed. Now Harry is being Mr. Big-Boots, bragging about what a fine sailor he is. I think he is quite sad that we are well again. The weather is still blowy and wet. Everything is grey. You can't tell where the grey seas end and the grey sky begins.

May 8

There was a concert in the second-class saloon and all the third-class passengers were invited. There was a pianist, a singing duet and a recitation of a funny poem about two blacksmiths and a rich merchant. Dad liked it especially because of being a blacksmith himself. After the concert he kept saying bits of the poem like, "He slept but was roused by the anvil's ring. And all day long it was ding, ding, ding," and, "If his daughter attempted to sing, The anvil accompanied, ding, ding, ding." Then Mother said she would ding ding him if he didn't leave off.

In my book Hector and Louis and Catharine found some partridge eggs and Catharine is boiling them for dinner. They are very clever about making a fire without matches. I'm trying to read slowly because we didn't bring many books with us. Lloyd has a couple of *Magnet* magazines he will lend me.

May 9

The captain of this ship is a fine gentleman. Today Dad and William were having a game of deck quoits and the captain walked by. He looks lovely, so polished and clean with a perfect black beard. He asked if he could join the game and then William won! Can girls be sea captains? If they can I would be one, just like ours. Friendly and not proud. (But I wouldn't like to have a beard.)

This evening William entertained the twins by reading them names from the map of Canada. "Moose Jaw" and "Medicine Hat" made them laugh so much they got the hiccups. Mother says it is all very well to laugh at Canadian place names, but remember, we come from a country that has places like "Wigglesworth."

May 10

Two more days until Canada. This morning I was at the stern looking over the rail and I had a funny idea. What if there is no Canada? What if there is no Moose Jaw or Medicine Hat or Piapot? What if we sailed and sailed and sailed and never reached Canada? What if Canada is a trick? All the map makers and globe makers and newspaper writers are in on the trick, and Uncle Alf too. Then we would end up in China. But what if China is a trick too? Looking at the wake makes your mind go peculiar like this.

The twins are starting to get a bit stroppy. I have to mind them this afternoon whilst Mother and Dad go out to play whist. Lloyd has to mind his little brother too, so we can get together for a game of ring toss.

Later

William made friends with one of the officers and he took him down to show him the ship's engine. Lucky. Mother is teaching me to knit. I try but my stitches just get tighter and tighter until I can't move them off the needles. I had to rip it all out and start over. Probably resourceful Catharine would knit with two twigs and a bit of grass or something. The writer of that book, Mrs. Traill, doesn't say when anything goes wrong.

It is very foggy.

May 11

This morning the fog cleared and there was Canada! Land ahoy! Canada isn't a trick after all. We are in the Gulf of the St. Lawrence River. It is very wide. Far away on both sides are mountains, woods, villages, puffs of smoke. I've seen some fishing boats but I haven't seen any Canadians yet. I told Gladys that it was Canada and she asked where Uncle Alf is. She doesn't understand how big Canada is.

I'm trying and trying to imagine the ranch. Is it like Wanstead Flats except with cows and horses?

Now it is time for our last meal on board. I hope they serve those scrumptious little crackers. Mother says I have to pack away this diary until we are on the train. She doesn't want me to lose it and likely I will because I'm such a scatterbrain. That's what Mother says. It's not fair. I'm not a scatterbrain. I just think about a lot of things at the same time.

Goodbye, *Ausonia*. Goodbye, port and starboard. Goodbye, bow and stern. Goodbye, lifeboats. Goodbye, Lloyd. Goodbye, our home on the waves.

Goodbye, lovely sea captain. Goodbye, captain's beard. Goodbye, dear diary. But just for a day.

May 12

Welcome back, diary. Quebec City was like Southampton. Crowds and piles of luggage and muddle. We took a taxi to the train station. The taxi driver was Scottish so we haven't met any real Canadians yet. Canadian trains are different. They have huge engines and corridors that go right down the middle. Ours is called a Colonist Car. It is divided into sections and because we are six we get a whole section. In the day the luggage is stored overhead in a sort of pull-down bin. At night the seats change to a bed and the luggage goes underneath and the overhead bin becomes another bed, with a little curtain over it. At the end of the car there is water and a stove for cooking.

I love sleeping on the train. It is like being rocked to sleep. NOT like the seasickness rocking of the ship.

May 13

Today Dad got out his *Canada West* booklet and read us bits. This is the booklet that tells us everything we need to know. It has a lovely coloured cover with a picture of a farmer holding an armful of grain in one hand and a fat baby in the other. The baby is holding a carrot as big as his head. First of all Dad read us the stories of people who got rich in Canada. One man arrived with 27¢ and now he has 200 acres of wheat and 20 cows. Another man made $5000 (that's more than £1000!) in one year fattening pigs. Then Dad told us what amusements there are in Canada, like hockey, football and tobogganing. I just can't wait for winter for snow.

The booklet said that "distance and isolation have disappeared" because of the radio. (That's Canadian for wireless.) I hope Uncle Alf has one. Then Dad read about how a man who has health, industry and good habits will be a sure success and how that sounded just like him. Mother snorted. He told us that luggage is called baggage, that a three-strand barbed wire fence costs $150 a mile and that there is absolutely no malaria in Canada.

Then William got larky and took over and read the tiny print on the inside of the cover that tells you who isn't allowed into Canada. They are vagrants, idiots and anarchists. (They forgot to say cats.) Harry said what's an anarchist. Mother said they blow things up and Harry said he wanted to be an anarchist. Dad said that was fine as long as nobody told the minister of immigration. The best words were "persons of constitutional psychopathic inferiority." This could be a useful insult. The twins practised saying it, over and over again, until Mother made them stop. Then they mouthed the words without saying them.

May 14

I just saw a bear! He was black and about the size of a fat man. He ran around behind a rock before I could tell the twins. I've also seen two kinds of birds with long necks. And a beaver lodge. The nice conductor told us about the beaver lodge. Otherwise I might have thought it was just a pile of sticks.

The conductor talks Canadian. He sounds like Ethel's uncle that came over from America.

This is not a pretty place. At least not in spring. There are big lumps of dead grass. It looks like the top of porridge when it is boiling. And patches of dirty snow. I can't imagine walking across it. Or living on it, like Catharine.

Catharine and the boys have been joined by their dog Wolfe. He found them. Maybe he will lead them home but I don't think so because the book isn't even half over.

May 15

Dear Diary,

We're STILL in Ontario. Ontario must be as wide as a whole big country. The sound of the train makes words go round and round in your head.

Lake, tree, tree, tree, rock, rock, tree.
Rock, rock, rock, tree, tree, rock, lake.

We just passed a lake that was as smooth as a mirror. If you hung upside down . . . Hey! If I went into the baggage car and hung upside down by my heels from the racks that lake would look exactly the same upside down as rightside up. I wish I COULD hang upside down in the baggage car. Or get a horse and ride beside the train. There I am, galloping along beside the train, waving to myself inside the train. Kuh-kuh-thunk, Kuh-kuh-thunk. Except the ground looks sort of boggy for galloping. The conductor said that the boggy stuff is called "muskeg." Canadian word. I wonder if they have muskeg in Saskatchewan.

May 16

It is very early and everything is different. Dad woke me up early and said, "Shhhh, keep your eyes closed." Then he put on my shoes. It feels very peculiar to have someone put on your shoes when your eyes are closed. Then he led me down the railway carriage. I heard somebody snoring and I got the giggles but I kept them inside. Then Dad opened the door and we went out onto the platform between the carriages. I could feel my feet shifting back and forth on the moving plates. Then Dad said, "Open your eyes." And I did, and, golly, everything was changed. The sun wasn't quite up but there was light and there were no rocks or trees or lakes, just huge fields. You can make your eye go as far as possible and nothing stops it. And flat. Flat as a table. I let the giggles out.

We didn't say anything for a while and it was like when we used to go for walks on Wanstead Flats after tea. Not talking. Just the two of us. It was the first time it had been just the two of us since England. Then Dad said, "Isn't it amazing? You can see clear through to half past tomorrow." We looked and looked. Then Dad started to hum. Sometimes he doesn't know that he's humming. But I knew the song. It was "What shall we do with a drunken sailor?"

I knew he was thinking of the sea — that the prairie was like the sea. He didn't need to say it.

Then we went back to the coach and Dad saw that nobody was using the stove yet, so he said he would start breakfast for us, and that I should go back to bed and coast until it was ready. So I'm back in bed, but writing, not coasting.

May 18

Winnipeg, Manitoba

We're on a new train. This line is called the Canadian Pacific. Everyone is asking why the train isn't leaving. We had a few hours in this city, which is called Winnipeg. At school there were two sisters called Winnie and Peggy Plumley. They should come and live here.

We went to a Chinese restaurant. I was a bit scared because I have never seen a Chinese person before and in *Magnet* magazine all the Chinese men have long moustaches and long knives. But it wasn't like that. In real life the Chinese restaurant man was just ordinary. Had a joke with the twins. The only knife he had was the one he used to cut the blueberry pie. Blueberry pie must be a Canadian food. It is lovely. The twins had blue mouths. We sat at a counter with red stools that twirled.

Then we went for a walk. We saw a sign on a livery stable that said, "Help Wanted. Englishmen Need Not Apply." Mother said wasn't that a fine welcome. I don't understand. In the *Canada West* book it says that Canadians want English people to come. What if nobody likes us? But that's rushing to meet trouble halfway and I'm not going to. It is probably just one grumpy livery man.

Anyway, the horses were lovely. I peeked in. But Mother said come along. I wanted to say, "Where does it say 'English Girls Need Not Peek?'" But I didn't because that would be cheeky.

First Chinaman. First blueberry pie. First twirly stool.

May 19

Somewhere between Maple Creek and Milorie

I am fit to burst. We are nearly there but it is taking forever. At Regina we switched trains to the mixed train. That means it takes people and freight. It also means it stops every eight miles at a town. Things get unloaded and loaded up and people stand on the platform and talk and talk and talk. This distance looks so little on the map but it is taking YEARS.

Still May 19

We made it. I used to be:

Ivy Doris Weatherall
107 Halley Road
Forest Gate, London
England
Europe
The World

and now I'm:

Ivy Doris Weatherall
Sec.1-6-26-W3rd
Uncle Alf's sod house
Five Miles from Milorie
Saskatchewan
Canada
North America
The World

The only thing the same is me and The World.

When we arrived at the train station in Milorie there were a lot of people on the platform. It took us a few minutes to find Uncle Alf. He was there with a team and wagon. A team means horses, not like the West Ham United football team. He gave us huge hugs and pretended not to know me because I was so grown-up and Mother cried a little bit. Auntie Millie and Baby Jack didn't come, because we would need all the room on the wagon for our things. Mr. Gilmour, a nice man called a station master, took us all home and his wife gave us tea and scones. Mrs. Gilmour said she made scones to make us feel at home because we are English. Mr. Gilmour told us that most of the people at the station had come down to look at us. "You're the big news in Milorie today," he said. I've never been news before.

Then we walked down the road and looked at the shops, which are a general store, two banks, a hardware store (that's Canadian for ironmongers), a garage, a livery stable, a blacksmith, and a doctor's office. Also there is a school and a church. The only tall buildings are two grain elevators. That's where they store wheat and that.

Then we all got on the wagon and we went along this dirt road full of ruts and the wagon went up and down and tippy and the two horses went plod plod. The twins went to sleep. How could they go to sleep when it is the most exciting day of our lives?

Dad asked Uncle Alf how many head of cattle he had and then I asked if he had a wireless. Then Uncle Alf got quiet and said that things in Canada weren't quite what they told you up at Canada House in London. Then he started to talk about the government and the railroad and politics and he sounded angry. But when he asked about all the relatives he got funny again.

William didn't sleep. He was excited too and he held my hand. Dad asked Uncle Alf where the pub was and Uncle Alf said there wasn't one and then Dad said, "What kind of godforsaken country have I come to?" and then Mother flicked him on the skull with her finger.

Then we got to Uncle Alf's house and it was a big surprise. We saw a wooden building, not painted at all, almost tumbledown, with rooms on either side made of sod. That's like dirt bricks. It has grass on the roof, like in the story of the silly woman who tried to put her cow up on her roof. I thought this was a shed for animals but I'm glad I didn't say so, because it is their real house!

When I thought of Halley Road and the flowers in the front garden and how Dad paints the front door every year I felt scared and homesick. I could tell that Mother and Dad were surprised too. Mother didn't say anything at all, and I saw her give Dad a look. But then Auntie Millie and Baby

Jack came out to greet us and there was more crying and more hugging and then more tea. Baby Jack is lovely. Then there were stories about all the aunts and uncles and cousins and Uncle Alf got silly and it was fine again.

William and I took the twins exploring. There is an outdoor privy and a barn. In the barn are chickens and a cow. Gladys found an egg! And when we took it back Auntie Millie said that I could milk the cow in the morning. The cow's name is Sally and she looks very friendly. I can hardly wait. At least part of the wait will be sleeping. I don't know where we will sleep because the shanty is small for six extra people. Maybe I can sleep up on the grass roof.

My hand is tired from writing. Today there is so much to say that I wish I had one of those typewriting machines that Auntie Lou has in her office in London.

Very last thing, a bit private. In the outhouse (Canadian word) there is a big catalogue from the T. Eaton Company. You can read it and then you tear out a page and use it for loo paper. Is that what everybody uses in Canada?

May 20

Banished to the Fields

(In *Lost in the Backwoods* each page has a title, like "A Weighty Consideration" or "Forest Dainties." I'm going to try it.)

All my life I've wanted to sleep out under the stars and last night I did! (But not on the roof.) Uncle Alf put a couple of straw mattresses out for William and me. The moon was so bright it made shadows. I kept waking up and wondering where I was and why I wasn't moving.

Chickens wake up very early. William and I went down the road a bit before anyone else stirred. We saw little furry creatures who pop out of holes and have a look round and pop down again. They are dear. I picked some flowers. (If I were Catharine I would know all their common and Latin names but I'm not and I don't.) When we got back I gave the flowers to Auntie Millie and she got sad and said they would die right away and how much she missed her rose garden at home in England.

She cheered up after breakfast and tried to teach me to milk Sally. It is much harder than it looks. I couldn't manage it. The cow kept turning her head and giving me a comical look.

Auntie Millie is very pretty. She has bobbed hair. I long to have bobbed hair. She told me that she used to take me for walks in my pram when I was a baby. She wanted to know all about home and had I been to the pictures and did I remember the fireworks on Halley Road at the Armistice Celebrations. She said she would give anything to put on a nice hat and take the tram into the centre of London and have tea at Lyons Corner House.

Lyons is jolly but I'd rather learn to milk Sally and drive a team.

After dinner Mr. Burgess who runs the general store arrived and everybody looked serious and Mother sent me away with the twins and Baby Jack. That's where I am now. Banished to the fields. Baby Jack can walk if you hold his hands. Harry and Gladys are making him laugh by pulling faces.

I wonder what is happening back at the house. Felt like some grown-ups-only secret when Mother shoved me out the door. William will tell me.

Later

I still don't know the secret — if that's what it is. Dad and Uncle Alf and William went off with Mr. Burgess in his wagon. And Mother, of course, isn't saying.

The creatures are called gophers.

May 21

The Truth About Uncle Alf

William told me everything. Uncle Alf doesn't have a ranch. He rents his farm. He owes money in every shop in town. Mr. Burgess has offered William a job working in the general store, but half his wages go toward paying off Uncle Alf's debts. Mr. Burgess has found us a house of our own to live in, because we certainly don't all fit in this one. So Mother and Dad said yes. The house is on a farm and we move tomorrow.

William isn't very happy. He wanted to be riding the range in Canada, not serving in a shop. Everybody is angry at Uncle Alf but I still like him. He calls Gladys "Glad-Eyes." He can walk on his hands and whistle at the same time. He did it this morning.

Mother did a wash today. Auntie Millie showed her how to do a wash in Canada. She said the water was so hard that you have to use lye so the soap works. Then she said how it makes your hands red and ugly. Then she had a little weep. Mother just said, "Never mind and wasn't it lovely drying weather."

May 22

A Mean Mother

I tried milking again today. Still can't manage it. Auntie Millie says, "Squeeze, don't pinch," but it doesn't work. Auntie Millie was nice about it though. She is nice, not like Mother. When I was carrying the pail of milk back to the kitchen I was just dancing a bit and I tripped and spilled half the milk. Later I heard Mother tell Auntie Millie that I was a flibbertigibbet. Then she said that if she and Dad had stopped with William they would have felt like perfect parents. Then she and Auntie Millie went laugh, laugh, laugh in a perfectly ROTTEN way. I am not a flibbertigibbet. It's just that Mother is so impatient and fast that she makes me make mistakes. I wanted to go climb a tree. At home when things are rotten I would always go to the cemetery and climb a tree. But there aren't many trees around Uncle Alf's. I miss home. I miss Grandad. He doesn't think I'm a flibbertigibbet. He thinks I'm a princess. I miss trees and Auntie Lou and Chivers and Ethel. Mother is mean. I'm going to write a letter to Ethel. No I'm not. Mr. Burgess has arrived with the wagon to move us.

May 22½

Weatherall Palace

Last night it rained so we had to move inside. It was a tight fit. Gladys and I had to sleep with our heads at opposite ends of the mattress. When everyone was lying down we couldn't open the door. I felt like a sardine.

But we aren't sardines anymore! We are in our own house. Auntie Millie cried when we left. The farm is called the Fretwell Farm. The Fretwells were an American family. Mr. Fretwell died in a farm accident and the rest of the family moved back to Minnesota. The house is lovely and big.

There is an upstairs with three bedrooms. There is some furniture like beds and a big kitchen table. There is a barn and a henhouse. There is also, of course, an outhouse — it's a two-holer. One hole is regular size and one is small. This is good because at Uncle Alf's Gladys was afraid of the outhouse. She thought she was going to fall down the hole.

I really wanted to play in the barn but I had to help unpack.

The first thing we unpacked was the gramophone. We kept winding it up and winding it up and playing the record we got for last Christmas, "I'm Forever Blowing Bubbles." Unpacking things made Mother much cheerier.

We had sausages for tea. For a treat we got to use the good cups and saucers. Even the twins. I still like the forget-me-not cup the best.

I'm writing this at the table. Dad is sitting in the rocking chair smoking his pipe. Mother has just wound up the gramophone again. It smells and sounds like home.

May 23

Ivy on Horseback

Today we had callers. They came in a wagon from a nearby farm. They were a lady named Mrs. Muller, a boy named Hans, and a girl named

Elizabeth. Mrs. Muller brought two saskatoon berry pies to welcome us to Canada. They were scrumptious. I don't think we have saskatoon berries in England.

Mother liked Mrs. Muller right away because she said her name was Gwyneth and Mother said was she Welsh and she said that her father was and then Mother said "So was my father" and then they just started talking and talking. Mr. Muller didn't come to visit. He's not Welsh. He's German.

Elizabeth is just my age. She likes to read. I told her about *Lost in the Backwoods* and she would like to borrow it when I'm done. She has a book called *Anne of Green Gables* that she is going to bring me. It sounds super. Now I don't need to make myself go slow with *Lost in the Backwoods*.

Elizabeth told me about school. There are only twenty-three students in the whole school and three of them are her and two of her brothers. She has four brothers and no sisters. Her brothers are Otto (2), Herman (6), Hans (13), and Gerhard (16). There is only one teacher for everyone. I said that would be terrible if you didn't like the teacher. I was thinking of Toad Eyes at home. Elizabeth said that it was because last year they had a horrid man who beat the big boys and frightened the little ones. But this year they have a nice teacher named Miss Hutchinson. I hope she stays until next year when I go to school. Elizabeth said Miss Hutchinson plays baseball with them at recess. (I didn't know what baseball was so Elizabeth told me. It sounds a bit like rounders.) This made me want to go to school right away, but Mother says there isn't any point so late in the year.

Elizabeth asked if I had been to Buckingham Palace to have tea with the king. I told her that ordinary people don't get to. Then she introduced me to the horse. Her name is Ruby. She is dark brown and as shiny as a conker. Elizabeth was amazed that I don't know how to ride. Then she just unhitched Ruby from the wagon and said did I want to get on. So I climbed onto the fence and then onto Ruby. Elizabeth said I should just hold onto her mane. She was higher and wider than I expected. Then Elizabeth led me around in a circle. It was lovely. My first time on a horse! I wanted everyone to see me. I wanted them to faint with astonishment. But nobody did and then Elizabeth hitched Ruby back up to the wagon. She is very good with reins and bridles and that. I think Elizabeth is resourceful and capable, like Catharine. I hope she would like to be my friend.

P.S. "Saskatoon berries" sounds like something in a nursery rhyme if you say it a few times.

May 25

Horses in Dreams and Dust

I dreamed about Ruby. I can just see myself riding off across the fields on her. Dad brought home the newspaper from Saturday. It is called the *Regina Leader* and it has a part just for kids called The Torchbearer's Club. My favourite part was the Magic Key Line Drawings. Here's how to draw a horse's head from a triangle.

I practised this over and over again in the dust in the yard. I think it looks just like Ruby. Next week is going to be a turkey from a circle. I wonder if Elizabeth likes to draw.

Dad got some work at the blacksmith's, but only for two days.

May 27

Butter Thoughts

Mother has a chance to buy a cow from the Mullers. We went over to their farm to see the cow and find out all about cows. Mrs. Muller is very kind and a good teacher. The cow is called Daisy and she is a soft brown colour with lovely eyes. Mrs. Muller asked me did I want to try milking and I said that I couldn't manage it and she said well of course I could and guess what? I did! It just worked, all of a sudden. I like the sound of the milk going into the pail, and the cow's warm side when I leaned against her. Gerhard came by and said that I was an English milkmaid.

There are kittens in the barn. Two black-and-white, two grey, and one marmalade, just like Chivers. They are very dear. I got to give them some milk. I wish we could have one.

Then Mrs. Muller told us about butter. Here is something I didn't know. Butter is made from cream and WORK. You take yesterday's cream and put it in this thing like a barrel, called a churn. Then you move a handle up and down and up and down and up and down and . . . until you think your arms are going to break off. Whilst you churn you say to yourself:

Come butter come
Come butter come
Peter standing at the gate
Waiting for the butter cake
Come butter come.

Elizabeth offered to help but I wanted to make butter all by myself. It takes about an hour but it feels like a week. Then finally the sound changes. Then you drain off the buttermilk (which is the milk without the butter; shouldn't it be called nobuttermilk?). Then you put water in the churn to wash the butter. When you take it out it looks like little lumps. You add salt with a paddle. This is fun. Churning is not fun.

When I used to have bread and butter for my tea at home I never wondered how butter was made. Mrs. Muller says that sometimes the cow gets into the stinkweed and then the butter is smelly and not worth eating. But this butter was lovely and well worth eating. I ate a lot on scones when we had tea.

Mr. Muller was out in the fields so we didn't get to meet him. The Mullers' house is quite grand. They have carpets on their floors. (Except they call them "rugs" and what we call "rugs" they call "blankets." Confusing.) It has a verandah that goes around three sides and stairs and a banister and a front door with coloured glass. You can stand close to the door on the inside and move back and forth and make the world go red green gold, red green gold, red green gold.

William started at the store today. It is two and a half miles for him to walk so he has to go very early. I can't wait for him to come home so I can tell him about milking and churning.

May 28

Mil-Orie

In my book Catharine and the boys have made a log cabin in the wilderness. It has a chimney, furniture and wooden dishes. Catharine is making clothes from animal skins.

William told me that Milorie got its name because one of the early homesteaders had two daughters named Mildred and Marjorie. So when he got to name the town he just combined their names. Marjorie still lives in Milorie. At home all the names of places are old, old, old. From Roman or Saxon times or something.

If we got to name a town from our names it could be Iviam or Gladarry.

May 29

Welcome, Daisy

Daisy has arrived. Now the barn really seems like a barn. Gladys and I made a flower crown for her.

What would Ethel say if she saw me milking and churning?

Yesterday night William told us all about his job. He cuts cheese and wraps it. He weighs out flour and sugar. He puts honey and molasses into containers. He puts raisins, biscuits and fruit into bags. When people bring in their cans he fills them with coal oil. He cleans the shelves. When people buy things he does the figuring and writes down the total in an accounts book. On Fridays he will get to go with Mr. Burgess down to the station to pick up supplies. They go with a horse and a big wagon with no sides called a dray. When William learns to drive horses he can do that himself. He says that all the Norwegian people buy this hard dried fish called *lutefisk*, and he told us about something called peanut butter which he says is absolutely scrumptious. He said most of the grown-ups are friendly but that some of the boys his own age say mean things to him, asking him why he talks so funny and that.

June 1

Cotton Confusion

I'm in trouble again. I think I was born under an unlucky star. It started when we went to visit Auntie Millie. Auntie Millie and Mother were sitting and talking and mending. Auntie Millie's mending basket was overflowing. I think Mother was trying to get Auntie Millie to buck up. Mother likes people to buck up and buckle down. Especially me.

But they ran out of cotton. Dad and Uncle Alf were going into town anyway so I went with them to go to the store and buy some. I was a bit shy to go into the store alone but I did. Dad and Uncle Alf went off to the livery stables to see about a job for Dad. (There wasn't one.) First thing I saw in the store was William. He was wearing a long blue apron and serving a woman and he didn't see me at first. Just for a minute he looked like a grown-up that I didn't even know. Then he saw me and grinned and he was himself again. If only he had served me. But he doesn't do that part of the store.

Instead it was Mrs. Burgess. When I asked for white cotton she said, "Plain white cotton?" I said yes, wondering if they have some fancy kind in Canada. Then she said, "How many yards?" This seemed like a funny question but I tried to be resourceful so I thought maybe they sell cotton by the yard in Canada, rather than by the spool, so I guessed and said, "Five yards." Then she reached up to a shelf and pulled down a bolt of white cloth! She began to unroll it on the counter. Wham! Wham! Wham! Then she took out a huge pair of scissors. I knew I should have said something but I got tongue-tied. She began to cut. The sound of the scissors made my blood run cold. Then she folded the cloth into a neat package and said, "Do you also need some thread, dear?"

Thread! That's what Canadians call cotton. All I could do was nod. Then she wrote it all in a book and I left.

I hid the cloth when I got to Auntie Millie's and

gave the cotton, I mean the thread, to Mother. What will happen at the end of the month when they go to pay the bill? I'll probably have to go to debtor's prison and live on scraps of bread and only have rats for company. This would never happen to Catharine. I wish I lived in the wilderness.

June 2

Summer in Saskatchewan

Did the milking this morning. Daisy likes me.

It is getting very hot. I love being warm all over completely. We are all turning brown. (Not Mother. She always wears a hat. She says we don't need to let our standards fall just because we're in the colonies.)

The cloth is hidden under my mattress.

June 3

Banana Trick

Some boys came in the store today and asked William for canned bananas. They waited until he got really confused and nervous because he couldn't find them, then they just laughed and left. There is no such thing as canned bananas. How was William supposed to know? At home we don't have bananas canned or any other way. Why are boys so mean? William says they think he is a toffee-nose, just because of the way he speaks. It is not fair. William is not a stuck-up person at all. I asked him if he wanted to quit the store. But he said that he can't because there isn't any steady work for Dad and we need the wages.

June 4

New Job

Dad and William have a new extra job. It is cleaning out the grain elevators in Milorie. They have to go in the bottom and scoop out the grain that is left over from last year so that the elevator is clean for this year's grain after the harvest.

June 5

Stinky Men

When Dad and William came home from the elevators Mother wouldn't let them in the house because they smelled so horrid. She made them wash in the barn. She said they smelled like the King's Head pub at closing time. At tea they told us about it. The grain is dirty and wet from the spring floods. And the space to work in is very small. The bottom part is called the boot. The tall part is called the leg. William says the work is like scooping up sludge. But the pay is good. William was so tired he went to bed before dark.

June 8

Hail the Conquering Chickens Come

The Weatherall family just got about eight times bigger. Fifty chickens have arrived. Edna Crank, the Chicken Lady, brought them. She is scary. She wears so many layers of clothes that you can't tell what the clothes used to be. Is that a kind-of-old cardigan or a really-old frock? Also, she is smelly. Also, she doesn't like children. When she looks at me I feel like she's wondering if I'm a good layer or what I'd be like plucked and roasted. But Mother says she knows everything about chickens and we have a lot to learn.

Here are some things we learned today:

1. If you whistle a tune when you go in the chicken yard the chickens go quiet.

2. Chickens are easy to fool. If they can't figure out to lay their eggs in the proper place (the nest box) you can give them the idea by putting china eggs into their nests. Maybe.

3. Do not feed them raw potato peels.

4. Warning: This is a bit horrid. Chopping off a chicken's head with an axe is not the best way to kill it. It will slap and twitch after it is dead, spattering blood around. The Chicken Lady just started to tell Mother how to dislocate a chicken neck using a broom handle when Mother said we were mostly interested in eggs. Thank goodness.

5. Chicken manure is very good for gardens. Of course Mother got all excited about this. Mother gets excited by very peculiar things.

The best thing about chickens is that they are comical. They run around, jigging back and forth and going "Braaaac, braaaac, braaaac," as though they have some terrible news to tell you RIGHT NOW. Whoever made up that story about Chicken Licken sure knew chickens. To me they are always saying, "Help, help, the sky is falling."

The Chicken Lady seemed to really enjoy telling Mother about loathsome things like chalky shell and sticktight fleas and the various forms of chicken cannibalism. When she said "vent picking" I stopped listening.

Finally the Chicken Lady said we should not name our chickens. "If you're going to eat it don't name it." But Harry started to anyway. Harry has just learned the alphabet and here is what he named the chickens:

Ahicken
Bhicken
Chicken
Dhicken
Ehicken
Fhicken

etc., etc. The flaw in his plan is that all chickens look alike, except for the rooster. You can't tell Qhicken from Whicken, even if they are part of the family.

June 9

First Chicken Morning

Woke up to the sound of the cock crowing. Whoever thought cocks said "Cock a doodle doo"? More like a rusty hinge on a door ending with the sound of somebody being strangled.

June 12

Letter from Home

Today I got a letter from Ethel. My first letter in Canada. She told me that there is a new family at 107 Halley Road and they yell a lot. Sometimes her father has to go next door and ask them to be quiet. Big news at school is that Toad Eyes has disappeared. There is a new maths master and nobody knows where Toad Eyes has gone. Ethel thinks either to hospital with a wasting disease or to prison for some dreadful crime. Chivers is just fine. There was a smudge on the bottom of the page that is a pawprint.

I started a letter right back to Ethel but there was so much that I needed to explain, just to tell her about chickens or anything. My hand got tired after a page. I wish I could just talk to her.

I'm thinking of the story of the country mouse and the city mouse. I used to be a city mouse like Ethel. I knew about the Underground, and feeding pennies in the meter for the gas and where the mummies are in the British Museum. But now I'm a country mouse and I know about milking and churning and chickens.

June 14

A Sneeze That Is a Show

Went into town today with Elizabeth's mother (and Ruby). We collected Elizabeth after school and went to the general store. A poster in the window had this strange word on it: Chautauqua.

I asked Elizabeth what it was and she said the word. It sounds like a sneeze. It is a kind of big show in a tent, with music and plays and lectures. Elizabeth says it is the best thing of the summer and I must come. It lasts for three days and there is a parade to start.

I finally got to see Elizabeth's father. He looks stern. He has lines down his cheeks and thick eyebrows that stick way out over his eyes.

June 15

Fiddlesticks

We're not allowed to go to the Chautauqua. It costs $2.25 for adults and $1 for children and Mother says that $8.50 would buy a lot of chicken scratch.

How can I get a dollar? I could churn butter and sell it to the store but one dollar is a lot of butter. Elizabeth says another way to make money is to kill gophers. You get one cent each for gopher tails, but mostly only boys do it. Even if I were a boy I would NEVER do it. It would be murderous blood money.

Oh. Just remembered. When I think about money, I think about the cloth under my mattress and the bill coming up at the end of the month.

June 16

Good News Day

We're going to the Chautauqua after all! Dad came home with tickets. Mother was a bit grumpy. But then Dad said that the Chautauqua is the poor man's university, brings the world to our door, and that we would remember it all our lives.

(Dad likes to say that we will remember something for the rest of our lives. If we remember all the things he says this about, we will spend the second half of our lives just remembering the first half. Once I asked Dad what he has remembered his whole life and he said that when he was a wee nipper he went to the opening of the Tower Bridge in London. It was opened by the Prince of Wales. He didn't remember the Prince of Wales. He remembered that when they raised the centre span of the bridge all the horse manure slid down the roadway.)

Mother got less grumpy when she looked at the programme. Some baritone singer is going to do opera. That was her first choice. William and I can go one day. The twins can go one day. We have to choose.

June 17

Parade

Today we went to the Chautauqua parade. It was children and animals. It was ever so funny. There was a marching drum band which was boys with dishpans. There were two boys on stilts. There were some small children riding hobby horses. There were all sorts of costumes like train conductor, clown and fairy. The animals were ponies, dogs, cats, a rabbit, two mice in a cage, and a pig. It was very muddling. The boy with the pig is called Abel Butt. The animals started off with costumes but mostly they got rid of them by the end. The pig in the baby bonnet just lay down in the road about halfway along and refused to move. So they moved him into a wagon pulled by boys pretending to be horses.

Everyone laughed.

Elizabeth told me the names of everyone. It was very muddling. One of the fairies was a very pretty girl called Nyla Muir. Elizabeth told me that she is a terrible show-off. I said was she a toffee-nose? Elizabeth didn't know what that meant, so I told her it means that you act so superior that your nose is stuck in the air. Elizabeth said that was a perfect description of Nyla.

Lots of the girls have bobs. I HAVE to get my hair bobbed before I start school.

At the end of the parade there was a group of children chanting the Chautauqua yell which goes:

C-H-A-U T-A-U Q-U-A
This is how you spell it!
Listen to us yell it!
CHAUTAUQUA!
CHAUTAUQUA!
CHAUTAUQUA!

Elizabeth wanted to just join in on the end of the parade but I felt too shy.

Whilst the parade was on, men were putting up a big brown tent in the field next to the school. Tomorrow the talent arrives and it really starts.

June 18

Deep Sea

Today was my day at the Chautauqua. That's it. I've decided. I'm going to be a deep-sea diver. William is too. Today we went to "The Bottom of the Sea" at the Chautauqua. Mr. Robert Zimmerman looks ordinary, like a bald Dad. But he has done amazing things. He competed in the Olympics and wrestled for his life with a deadly shark. (Not at the Olympics. At the Olympics he was in the swimming competition.) If you have even one little cut on your body sharks smell the blood and go for you. He dived for the sunken treasure of the last Spanish galleons. He helped make the picture *Twenty Thousand Leagues Under the Sea.* I would give anything to see that picture. He talked about seas as warm as a bathtub, and huge manta rays, and water that shines in the dark, and rainbow-coloured fish and octopusses.

After the lecture part of the talk he asked if we had any questions. Toffee-Nose was there, wearing new hair ribbons. Some people ask questions because they really want to know something. And some people ask questions because they want to show off. Toffee-Nose is the second kind of someone.

After the questions everyone got to go up on the platform and look at all the sea things. There were barracuda teeth, sea sponges, stuffed fish, a turtle shell (so big that you could hide Baby Jack under it), shells, starfish, beautiful coral and all Mr. Zimmerman's diving equipment.

On the way home William and I started to talk about the *Ausonia*, about how much was going on in the water under the ship and we never thought about it. There we were, floating along, and under us was a whole world, miles straight down of swimming, eating, attacking fish families, and jellyfish dancing. I also thought of a question, too late. If you are standing in Milorie, Saskatchewan, Canada, and you hold a shell to your ear and you hear the sea, what sea are you hearing? Anyway, William and I are going to be the deep-sea diver brother-and-sister team and we're going to discover many new kinds of fish and along the way we'll pick up some sunken treasure to get the money for our expeditions.

June 19

People on Strings

Today the twins got to go to the Chautauqua. It was a marionette show. Dad and I met the twins at the end and they told us all about Jack and the Beanstalk. Harry said that he wasn't afraid of the giant because he only smelled the blood of an Englishman, and he wasn't an Englishman anymore, but a Canadian. Then Dad said, "So I suppose you don't want your tea then because Canadians don't have tea, only supper." And Harry said, "I shall have my tea and call it supper," and then Dad pretended to box his ears. Then Harry and Gladys recited "and he climbed and he climbed and he climbed and he climbed" and so on, all the way home, until Dad and I had to run ahead with our fingers in our ears. I wish I could go to the Chautauqua every day. Every day until I grow up and become a deep-sea diver.

June 21

Family Expands Again

Baby Jack has come to live with us. Mother brought him back from Uncle Alf and Auntie Millie's. He is sleeping in a drawer at the end of my bed. He is making a tiny little popping sound as he sleeps. I'm not supposed to know why he's here, but I do. I heard Mother telling Dad. There's a hole in the floor where the heat comes up in winter but the sound of voices comes up all year long.

(True confession: Actually you have to lie on the floor and put your ear to the grate, which I happened to be doing.)

Mother went to visit Auntie Millie and when she got there Auntie Millie was just lying on the bed and staring and Baby Jack was crying and his nappy hadn't been changed in ever so long. Mother says that Auntie Millie is sick but I know it isn't like the flu or something. Mother says Auntie Millie should never have left England, that she isn't the pioneer sort. But then Dad said that living with someone like Uncle Alf would drive anyone round the twist, what with the lies and the debts. Then Mother got quiet. After all, Uncle Alf is her brother. I wouldn't like anyone to say bad things about William.

I wonder if Auntie Millie would like to read *Lost in the Backwoods*. It says, "To be up and doing is the maxim of a Canadian; and it is this that nerves his arm to do and bear." Isn't that good? It makes me feel all holy, like hymns or "God Save the King."

In *Lost in the Backwoods* Catharine and the boys have built themselves sleds and are whizzing down hills. I CAN'T WAIT for winter and snow. There's a good hill out by the coulee.

Mother and Dad had words before tea. Mother said, "Now that we have Jack to take care of we absolutely need to buy a copper to boil the nappies." (We didn't bring our copper from home because it was too big and heavy.) Then Dad said that we couldn't afford to buy a copper because we needed to save for shoes and that. (Then I remembered the secret under my mattress. But I cast the thought from my mind.) Then Mother got cross. But it all turned out to be for nothing because Elizabeth's mother came over and told Mother that they don't boil nappies in Canada. They just peg them out and the prairie sun bleaches them. Too sleepy to write more.

June 23

Flying Jack

I'm in trouble again. I took Baby Jack over to Elizabeth's house and we were playing with him and Otto. Peepo and that. (In Canada they call it peekaboo). Then we got this idea to put them in a flour sack and give them swings. It worked fine with Otto. And at first it was fine with Baby Jack. He loved it. He made this hiccup noise he makes when he's really happy. But then the bottom of the flour sack ripped open and Jack went flying through the air, headfirst into the Mullers' chiffonier. He got a nosebleed and quite a lot of blood got onto the doilies on the chiffonier. And of course he cried a lot. I felt awful.

At least we're both in trouble. It's not quite so bad being in trouble with a friend. And Mrs. Muller is pretty nice. Truth to tell, it was my idea but Elizabeth took half the blame.

Mrs. Muller put Mercurochrome on Jack's wounds. I thought perhaps we could bind them with cooling leaves of tacmahac, like Catharine does in *Lost in the Backwoods*, but Mrs. Muller thought Mercurochrome would be better. And she told me that if the blood doesn't come out of the doilies she'll teach me to tat and I can make new ones.

At least Jack doesn't blame me. He sat on my lap all evening and held onto my ear.

June 25

Sir Lancelot

William has rescued me. He is like a knight in shining armour. I was so worried about the cotton/thread that I finally told William. He told Mrs. Burgess and she just laughed and said that I should bring back the cloth (I mean the cotton; I'm going to practise saying everything Canadian so I don't get in trouble again) and that she wouldn't charge us and that Mother never need know. I am so relieved that I feel like a bouncing ball. When we are deep-sea diving and William is in the sucking clutches of an octopus I will save him, even though the sharks are coming right at me with teeth bared. I promise.

June 27

Bad Words

Today we went to church. (Well, not Dad. He's not much for church). The vicar's name is Mr. Quigley, but he is called a minister. He's not old. Church is a bit plainer than at home but the words are the same.

The Mullers were there. And that toffee-nose girl and her parents.

After church I was standing outside with Elizabeth and Toffee-Nose. Harry and Gladys started racing around people's legs, singing hymns in their private language, so I said, "Stop that, you silly asses." All the grown-ups turned around and looked at me. Then Toffee-Nose made her mouth into a drawstring and said that I shouldn't use bad language, especially not on the sabbath. Then she walked away.

That is so unfair. At home "ass" isn't such a bad word. I mean it is a little bad, but not really bad. Mother says it all the time when Dad does something like singing pub songs. I even heard the VICAR say it at home.

How are you supposed to know these things? That book for new immigrants that tells you all about farming and that — it should have a section on words, bad and otherwise.

July 1

July the first was a day of firsts for Ivy Doris Weatherall but I am too tired to write about it so I will tomorrow.

July 2

Best Day in Canada

I couldn't write about yesterday yesterday because yesterday had too much in it. It was Dominion Day, a holiday for the Dominion of Canada. It was the day of the Milorie community picnic. Dad woke me up by standing at the door singing "The Maple Leaf Forever." I got teary. I always get teary when I hear songs like that. It's like the sound goes in my ear and then behind my eyes, pushing the tears out. William says I'm a wet silly. I don't care. Dad was singing "The thistle, shamrock, rose entwine, The Maple Leaf forever," when Mother walked by and said, "And what about the leek?" She means the Irish get the shamrock, the Scots get the thistle, and the English get the rose, but where's the Welsh leek. Mother always stands up for the Welsh. Dad grabbed her round the waist, even though she was holding Baby Jack. Then he did moony-eyes and sang, "The leek and rose by love entwined, the Weatheralls forever," which made Mother laugh though she pretended not to.

Everyone was in a jolly mood because of the picnic. We did the milking and collected the eggs. Then I helped Mother make ginger cookies and hard-boiled eggs and then we all walked over to the Muller farm. Everyone was there. They came out from town in wagons and buggies and on horseback and some in cars. (They parked their cars near the barn. This is an important thing to know because of what comes later in this story. I am building suspense.) The men set up tables under the poplar trees and then the food started to appear. Everybody shared. There were raisin buns in a ring, and cinnamon buns (Harry and I like to unwind cinnamon buns as we eat them, which saves the best sugar bit for last; Elizabeth and William like to take bites with every part at once; Gladys just likes to eat hers as fast as possible any which way), doughnuts, ginger cookies, molasses cookies and railroad cake. Something I had never had before was raw cabbage with a sauce on it. I asked Elizabeth what the sauce was and she said, sour cream, mustard and sugar, which I thought sounded horrid. Sour cream! But I tried some and it was delicious. Sour cream in Canada doesn't mean the same thing as sour cream at home. There was cold chicken and cold sliced ham and something called vinegar pie which also sounds horrid but isn't. Also butter tarts which sound lovely and are. The biggest surprise was a box of oranges and bananas. At home we only get oranges at Christmas. When I put a piece of orange in my mouth I felt really peculiar. I felt like I should be hearing "Hark the Herald" and holding cold hands up to the fire. When the bananas were handed around I paid close attention to Elizabeth because I've never had a banana and it is hard to know how to get into a banana if you've never had one. A very tidy fruit but I didn't think much of the taste. A bit like glue. And there was lemonade too, in a big washtub with a block of ice.

We ate until we were stuffed. Then the grown-ups had a rest or played horseshoes. Then there were games. I entered the running race for girls and two races that I had never heard of before. In the sack race you hop along in a potato sack. In the three-legged race you tie one of your legs to one of your partner's legs with a piece of rag and then you run like one person with three legs. I was a partner with Elizabeth. We tried to sing "Pop Goes the Weasel" so that we would have a rhythm. It didn't work. We got tangled up and fell over and then we couldn't stand up because we were laughing so hard.

The Weatherall family did not triumph in the races. We would have gone home without a single ribbon if it were not for Mother. She won the ladies' nail-driving contest. I think the ladies' nail-driving contest is supposed to be a sort of funny thing. There is a lot of chivvying that goes on before. Two long boards are laid along the ground, one on top of the other. The women kneel in a long line along the edge of the board. They each have a hammer and five nails. Somebody says "Mark, Set, Go!" and they all start nailing. There is a lot of teasing and some ladies just give little ladylike taps, but Mother went at it very seriously. I could tell she wanted to win. And she did. Wham, wham, wham. First prize. Then all the men started saying would she come and build them a henhouse and things like that but Mother just pinned on her ribbon and smiled.

Then the men made ice cream in a big freezer. They each took a turn cranking. The ice cream would have been the best thing of the day except for something that came later. (I am building suspense again). Then there was a baseball game. Abel Butt, the boy with the pig in the parade, ran all around the bases in one go. That's called a "home run." He did a cartwheel at the end. (That's not part of baseball.) William joined in but even though he is a good cricket batsman he "struck out." It made him a bit sad.

For supper we ate more of everything.

When it was almost finished Mrs. Muller was pouring a last cup of coffee from the big coffee kettle and she said, "What's this?" and then she pulled this soggy thing out of the kettle. She wrung it out and it turned out to be a grey sock. Then everyone came over to see and Mr. Quigley said it looked like his sock and Mrs. Quigley said that it was, that she had knitted it and that it had been missing from the line last wash day. Then everyone said, how could it have gotten into the coffee? Then Mr. Quigley said at least it was clean when it went in! Then he started to sing "Who put the overalls in Mrs. Murphy's Chowder?" and Dad joined in. What the adults didn't notice was that Hans Muller and another big boy were out behind the wagons rolling on the ground laughing.

Then we went to the Mullers' barn for a dance.

The music was two fiddles and an accordion and the dances were square dances. I don't know how to dance but I liked leaning on the horse box and listening to the music and feeling the floor shivering. I liked seeing the dust floating up and hearing Jimmy Snook telling the dancers what to do. "Places all, hit the lumber with your leather." "Bow to your corner." "Grand chain." "Circle stags and Do-si-do." I noticed that sometimes he would say "Promenade your partner home," then the next time he would say, "Take your gal to you know where." Or put somebody's name into it. It was like on-the-spot poetry. I would like to know how to dance Canadian dancing.

This next part is extra private. All snoopers keep out.

July 3

Going for a Spin

I got too tired to write this yesterday and I was running out of ink anyway. Back to Dominion Day.

It was hot in the barn and the twins and Baby Jack went to sleep almost right away, lying on a pile of straw. I was nearly asleep too when William came over and whispered that I should come with him. We went outside, around the corner of the barn and there was Hans sitting in the Mullers' Model T. "Want to go for a spin?" he said. Hans is only thirteen years old. I asked him if he was allowed to drive and he just gave me a big wink. I knew it was naughty but I wanted to go SO MUCH so I said yes. Besides I figured that if we got into trouble William would get into bigger trouble than me. So I got in and Hans and William started saying things like spark lever and throttle lever and how you could break your wrist if the car backfired whilst you were cranking. Then Hans cranked and the motor started and both boys jumped in and we were off. My first ride in a private car. It was lovely lovely lovely. I could hardly breathe for being so happy. When Hans really "opened up" (that's car talk for going fast) we must have been going thirty miles an hour. It felt as fast as the train except instead of being cooped up and tied to the track you can look up to the sky or down to the weeds along the side of the road which are WHIZZING by. If you put your cupped hand out you can scoop up air like water. It was like flying, but bumpier. Every bump made us whoop. We went down the road a piece and then back. I wanted to go all the way to Milorie, to Regina, to the North Pole! Most of all I would love to drive a car myself. When we got back nobody noticed except some men who were around the back of the barn passing around a bottle and they didn't seem very interested.

So that was the first of July and the first of banana eating and the first of running three-legged and the first of going to a square dance and the first of riding in a car.

July 5

The Slew

This morning the twins took all the lids off the stove and hid them. Then they disappeared. Mother came in from the garden to make a cup of tea and there was the stove, full of holes.

She did finally find twins and lids but she said I had to mind them for the afternoon whilst Baby Jack was napping. I took them down to the slew. The slew is like a pond, where all the kids swim. We all had a splash round. We don't know how to swim because we were only at the seaside once, with Auntie Lou, and it rained the whole time. Not hot hot hot like here. I would rather mind the twins than weed in the garden, or, worse, pick off potato bugs.

July 9

Ivy Weatherall: Horsewoman

I rode Ruby again. Elizabeth came over and we had a lesson in the yard. This time I held the reins myself. Who do I love best? Daisy, Ruby or Chivers?

July 15

Zowie

We get to go to the fair in the Mullers' car! Flying all the way to Stanton. Eight miles! Mr. and Mrs. Muller are going with the wagon but Gerhard is going to drive the Model T and take me and Elizabeth. Hurray! Hurray! O frabjous day. How can I stand to wait a whole week and one day? (Reminder to myself: Remember to pretend that this is my first ride in a car.)

July 16

Toad Tale

Gerhard Muller is a toad. A toad of toads. This morning I was under Elizabeth's front porch with Elizabeth. We didn't go down there to eavesdrop. We were there before Toad Gerhard and Worm Emily Piggott even came onto the porch. Emily was supposedly at the Mullers' to help Mrs. Muller make pies. But Elizabeth says she's sweet on Gerhard and he's sweet on her and that's why she comes over so often. Toad-Gerhard and Worm-Emily started talking about the fair and the first thing we hear is Gerhard inviting Emily to join him in the Model T. Emily said that would be "looooovely." (How come Gerhard doesn't notice how silly Emily sounds? I think being sweet on somebody is like some sort of influenza that causes a person to be stupid.) Then Emily said how much more "looooovely" it would be if they would travel to the fair alone, just the two of them. So Gerhard hemmed and hawed and then he said that he would think of a way to get rid of the nuisances. NUISANCES! That's the very word he used. Elizabeth and I were so mad that we could hardly keep quiet. But we did. Which was good. Because now we can plan our secret revenge.

July 17

A Brilliant Plan

I've got it. I got the idea from Dhicken. Dhicken is the chicken who won't lay her eggs in the henhouse. She lays them all over the yard and they are usually cracked and broken. This morning when I was hunting for those eggs I got my idea. I told Elizabeth. She says I am brilliant. And tomorrow is Sunday and that means Gerhard will be going over to the Piggott place to see Emily.

Perfect.

July 18

In the Doghouse

Elizabeth and I are in the doghouse. Who would have thought that Gerhard was not only a toad but a snitch? My punishment is that I have to clean the henhouse for a whole week by myself. Elizabeth's punishment is that she has to weed the whole garden. Our punishment together is that we don't get to go to the fair in the Model T, but only in the wagon like everybody else. (How do mothers think of these punishments? Do they have a secret book somewhere?) But here's a secret, dear diary: I would do it again in a minute.

This afternoon after church and dinner Elizabeth and I hung around Gerhard whilst he groomed Ruby and cleaned all the harness and polished his boots. We were nice as pie but all the time we were thinking, "nuisance, nuisance, nuisance." Then when he went off to change his clothes and slick back his hair and all that, we disappeared. We went out to a field along the road to the Piggott place. What did we have with us? My lunch pail full of cracked eggs.

One funny thing: Mrs. Muller told everyone that we wouldn't be mentioning this to Mr. Muller. They have a lot of secrets in that family.

Just one more thing: Mother asked me why I'm always getting into trouble with Elizabeth. Then she said why don't I make friends with a nice girl like Nyla Muir. Which proves to me that grownups don't know a thing about what's going on. They ain't got the sense they was born with. (That's not bad grammar. It is from a story.)

July 21

A Plan

Elizabeth and I have decided to enter Junior Jams and Jellies at the fair. Elizabeth says she has a secret weapon. Toffee-Nose won Junior Jams and Jellies last year (and Junior Pies Two Crusts) but this year Elizabeth says she better watch out.

July 22

The Secret Weapon

Today we made our junior jelly. It is crabapple. It was fun to make except for the wasps who got into the kitchen and tormented us. My favourite part was when the jelly starts to drip. You turn one chair over on another (seat to seat) and you tie a hot wet tea towel to the legs of the chair so that it makes a sort of bag. Then you put a bowl under the bag. Then you pour the crabapple pulp into it and wait. It is SO tempting to squeeze the bag and make it go faster but you absolutely mustn't or the jelly will go cloudy. The secret weapon is beet juice. Elizabeth boiled some beets and then she took the bright red beet water and put some into the crabapple pulp. It was her own invention, to make the jelly really rosy.

Everything worked perfectly. Our jelly is a beautiful colour, it isn't one bit cloudy and it jelled perfectly. Mrs. Muller says that if it doesn't jell you just call it sauce but there is no Junior Sauce prize. We're off to the fair!

July 24

Defeat

Phooey. Guess who entered Junior Jams and Jellies? Guess who entered with crabapple jelly, just like us? Guess who cut little circles of gingham cloth with her pinking shears to make little bonnets for her jelly jars? Guess who won first prize? The answer to all of the above questions is a girl whose initials are N.M., also known as Toffee-Nose. I think she won for her bonnets, not for her jelly, which wasn't nearly as beautiful as ours. We won third prize.

The fair was fun, though. Mrs. Muller won a prize for her quilt. There was a new kind of threshing machine that had all the men admiring it. I wanted to look too but the salesman was a grump. "No kids around here," he said.

We did get to ride home in the Model T. I guess we are forgiven.

Good thing about Canada: bare feet. Dusty roads are very soft.

July 25

Something to Remember

Today it was very hot and Elizabeth was busy and the twins were speaking their secret language and I told Mother that I was bored. So she sent me to the neighbour's field to collect meadow muffins. Meadow muffins are cow manure. You dry them and then you can burn them in the stove. This is a completely horrid job. The thing to remember is never never say to Mother that I am bored.

July 27

A Sad Day

This afternoon Mother and Dad took Jack over to Uncle Alf's. When they came home they had no Jack and bad news.

Uncle Alf and Auntie Millie and Baby Jack are going home to England. Mother wrote to Millie's people and told them about Auntie Millie being sad and sick, and Uncle Alf owing all the money and all that. So Auntie Millie's father sent them the fares to go home. They are leaving on Thursday.

There is an empty place in the house where Jack used to be. I will miss him.

July 28

Farewell

They all came for supper this evening. Dad got some beer for himself and Uncle Alf but it wasn't a jolly party. Uncle Alf was too quiet. The twins behaved very badly and Mother blew up at them and said, "Is this the way you want your aunt and uncle to remember you?"

Uncle Alf is going to work for Auntie Millie's father. He makes prams.

After supper Uncle Alf did tease a bit. He asked me if I wanted to go with them, and said that he was sure they could find a hidey-hole on the ship. For a minute I wanted to say yes. Not because of Grandad or Ethel or even Chivers. It was because of the cupboard under the stairs on Halley Road. I used to go there to hide. It smelled like boot polish.

Baby Jack is teething and he was grizzly so I took him outside and played peepo and tickle-under-the-chin. He snuggled right in and held my ear and said, "I-bee." That's his way of saying Ivy. I cried a bit when I thought that he might be a grown-up man before I saw him again. Then he put his hands over my eyes and made his bubble noise with his mouth. He was trying to cheer me up.

It is going to be strange in Canada with no relatives. Empty.

August 2

Kitten Surprise

Today we found out about a Canadian animal. Gladys and I were helping Mother hang out laundry this morning when Harry came around the corner of the house and said, "Look, I've found a kitten."

Mother was just saying, "Well, that's all we need, a cat," when she turned to look and there was Harry standing with a skunk in his arms.

Mother froze and then she said in a very low calm voice, "Just put the kitten down, Harry." But then Harry said, "Can't I keep it? Can't I keep it?" jumping up and down. Before anybody could do anything the skunk gave a wriggle and sprayed Harry.

I've smelled faint skunk on the breeze before, but skunk close up is different. It is absolutely disgusting. It is like having something sweet and horrid stuffed up your nose.

Harry yelled and dropped the skunk. The skunk ran away in a hurry.

Mother put Harry and all his clothes in the washtub in the yard and scrubbed them but Harry still has a terrible pong.

Gladys was eager for Harry to get into trouble but Mother says how was he to know about skunks. He knows now.

August 3

Jam for Wages

Dad has another job. He's working with the railway crew who repair track. He doesn't get paid with money, but they give him food. Today he came home with a HUGE pail of strawberry jam.

August 7

Traitor

I hate William. I hate and detest and loathe him and I am never going to speak to him for the rest of my life. This I vow and promise and I won't go back on it ever. He is a sneak and a loathsome vermin.

Today I went to town with Dad. I was supposed to go to Bill Bowler the butcher to get the free liver. (Canadians don't like to eat liver and kidney so Bill Bowler gives it to us for free.) I was walking by the general store and there was a bunch of boys larking about the back door. They were all carrying gopher tails and waiting to collect their money from Mr. Burgess. I hardly looked at them. I hate seeing those bloody tails. You know what they do, dear diary? They pour water down the holes and when the gophers come up they bash them on the heads. Those little faces and the way they pop up and look around. The farmers say they eat the grain. I DON'T CARE. There is lots of grain. There is grain till half past tomorrow. The gophers can have some.

Anyway, the way those boys were laughing I knew they liked killing the gophers, they liked being murderers. Boys are horrible.

And William is ONE OF THEM.

He was there. With those boys. With gopher tails in his hands. With the murderers. He didn't see me. I ran away as fast as I could. And then I looked down at the package of liver in my hands and blood was leaking out of it so I threw it over the fence into the Battrum's yard. Then I had to climb over the fence and go get it, because that's what we're having for tea.

From this day forward, now and forevermore, William Walter Weatherall is not my brother and so I sign in blood.

Later in the Day

Dear Diary, I take it back. I can because I didn't sign in blood after all. I tried to pull the scab off my knee to get some blood but it hurt too much. Then I went down to the kitchen to get some liver blood but Mother was already cooking it.

Here is what happened. I didn't speak to William at tea. I treated him with cold disdain. But nobody noticed. Mother was talking about the cutworms who ate her lettuce. Then the twins started speaking their secret language and pretending not to know English, which makes Mother furious, and there was a big row. I felt like I was wasting my disdain.

But then after tea I went to the outhouse and there was William, behind it, vomiting. He was white as milk. And he was blinking. He has been blinking a lot since we came to Canada. And he looked so miserable and white and blinky that I forgot my vow of silence and asked him what was what. He put his head under the pump and then we walked away from the house, where no twins could find us, out to the coulee.

He told me how much he hated killing the gophers, how they bleed when you bash them but how if he didn't go kill gophers he wouldn't have any friends. He says all the boys hate him because he is English and they say he talks funny and he doesn't know how to swim and they call him "Dirty Will" because of the elevator cleaning job. So he pretended to like killing gophers. But he said that he's not going to do it anymore. He said, "I'll learn to swim and I'll talk like a Canadian, but I'm not going to do any more killing."

I asked him how much money he got from the gophers. He said fifteen cents but he gave it away to Daft Binnie who sits in front of the livery stables. He said I was his only friend and I felt bad that I wrote that he was a loathsome vermin. At least he didn't know. Sometimes it is better to insult people in a diary than to their face.

I feel really sad that William doesn't have any friends. Elizabeth Muller doesn't mind that I don't talk Canadian. She likes it when I say treacle and nappies and tea instead of syrup and diapers and supper. I think it is harder being a boy. I'm glad I'm not one.

I asked William if he wanted to go home to England but he said that he didn't because in England he would never get to be anybody in particular, but here he was going to be somebody. He sounded very fierce. Walking back to the house I wondered if I was going to be somebody. I've never thought of that before.

August 10

A Beating from the Sky

I'm writing this in bed. My fingers are the only part of me that doesn't hurt. Gladys is beside me, asleep. We have two hot water bottles.

Early this morning we went out to the coulee to pick saskatoon berries. We nearly had our pails full when all of a sudden it got really dark, like somebody had thrown a cloth over the sun. And hail started falling, faster and faster, big hailstones like walnuts. It was hitting the ground and bouncing back. There was nowhere to hide. Gladys started screaming so I grabbed her hand and we tried to run. But the hail was icy cold and slippery and when we got to the road Gladys fell down and she couldn't get up. I tried to shelter her but the hail was coming from all directions. I don't know how long we were there but then the Chicken Lady appeared. She took off one of her jackets and held it over us. And finally finally finally it stopped. But we still couldn't walk because our feet were icy cold and blue and the hail was deep. The Chicken Lady told me to ride piggyback and she picked up Gladys and carried us home. Her big boots went crunching on the hail. The only part of me that wasn't freezing was my front on her back. Too tired to write more.

August 10, later

I fell asleep before I put the pen down and now ink has leaked onto the quilt.

The rest of the story is that halfway to home Mother came and found us and took Gladys. When we got home we couldn't stop shivering. Mother put us to bed. When I was trying to protect Gladys from the hail I thought we were both going to die. I don't want to think about this anymore.

August 10, after supper

Gladys and I had supper in our nightgowns. Everyone talked about the hailstorm. It wasn't everywhere but some farmers lost whole fields of grain. One farmer said that his fields looked like summer fallow. Then William told a story that he heard at the store. He said that one of the Butt family's pigs was out of the barn and when they got to her she was pulling herself along on her front legs because her back was broken by the hail. When William said this I remembered Abel Butt's pig in the bonnet at the Chautauqua parade and then I wondered if it was the same pig and then I just started to cry and shiver and I couldn't stop. Dad took me on his lap even though I'm too big and Mother made me drink two cups of sweet tea.

Gladys asked what happened to the pig and William said the farmer had to kill it. I know that pigs are killed. I know what bacon is. But I wish I didn't have that picture of the pig in my mind. I would like to take a rubber and erase the whole thing, pig, hail, Gladys crying. Now I'm tired again.

August 11

I ache all over. Gladys and I both have blue bruises on our legs and arms. The hail is all melted and outside it just looks like ordinary summer again. But part of me thinks it is a trick. Mother says I am excused from chickens today. Gladys and I are going to help make a cake for the Chicken Lady to thank her.

This is the most *Lost in the Backwoods* thing that has ever happened to me.

Mother wasn't angry about the quilt. She said that she will teach me how to take out the inky piece and put a new piece in.

August 16

Hair Ribbon Hatred

I'm not allowed to get my hair bobbed. Mother says I'm too young and she doesn't want me to look like a flapper. I'll probably be the only eleven-year-old girl in school who still wears hair ribbons. I said that all the girls I have seen in Milorie, except for little ones, have bobs. She said if all the girls jumped down the well, would I? She wants me to be miserable.

August 17

Wrongly Blamed

I'm in trouble again. If I had one of those printing sets I would just make up those words and print them in this diary every time I got into trouble, which is always.

It started because William dropped a tin of lard onto his foot. And his big toe was all swollen and red and horrible looking. And I remembered something from *Lost in the Backwoods*. There's this bit where Catharine sprains her ankle and Louis and Hector take some strawberries and crush them and apply them to her ankle as a "cooling poultice." Nobody was home and William was limping around and then I remembered the big tin of strawberry jam that Dad had earned on the railway. And I figured that strawberry jam must be just about the same as crushed up strawberries. So I took some and made William sit in the front yard with one foot up on a chair. I covered his toe with jam. In the book they put on the poultice with oak leaves and bind it with strips of bark. I used caragana leaves and string. Then, "rendering the application even more generous," just like Louis and Hector, I got William a drink of water and went inside to put away the jam.

Next thing I know I hear a yell and I look out the window and there is William dancing all over the yard and beating at the air and then Mother comes home. Turns out that the jam attracted wasps and they were stinging William and now he has wasp stings as well as a swollen toe. Mother got very angry at me and she thought the swollen toe was from the wasps as well. I said, "That's not wasps, that's a tin of lard." But nobody was listening to me.

These are my crimes:

1. wasting food
2. causing my brother to be stung by wasps
3. answering back *

That's it. I'm not going to try to be resourceful anymore. If I had had proper oak leaves and moosewood bark it probably would have worked fine. That's my last poultice. I think I'll go live in the wilderness.

* The answering back is when I said, "Well, it is just a wasp sting. Not the Great War." Things just pop out of my mouth before I can stop them.

August 18

Halleluiah

I am the happiest girl in Saskatchewan or maybe the world. I have a horse. Mr. Burgess found a horse for us because Mother and Dad thought it would be too far for the twins to walk to school. Her name is Dot. She is dappled grey. She has very soft lips and already I love her.

Mr. Burgess gave us a lesson and he said I was a quick learner. (He didn't know that I had already practised on Ruby). Then Gladys and Harry tried and they didn't fall off. I asked if we were going to have a saddle but Mr. Burgess said that saddles are too dangerous for children. What if the horse bolts and the children fall off but they get caught in the saddle and are dragged. I don't understand why this is more dangerous than falling off on your head. But I don't care about a saddle. I have a horse!

I found out everything about caring for her. She has to be combed and brushed and have her hooves waxed with floor wax. She eats oats twice a day and hay and water. When we take her to school we keep her in the school barn and we take her dinner with us.

Harry said could he gallop and Mr. Burgess said he wasn't ready yet and besides he had his doubts about whether Dot could gallop. He called her a steady, reliable school horse. But I think she is a noble steed.

Mother is happy because of the manure for her garden. Of course.

August 25

Thoughts on Mosquitoes

I'm nearly at the end of *Lost in the Backwoods*. (I stopped for a while because Elizabeth lent me her *Anne of Green Gables*. It was swell.) Catharine has been captured by Indians. Louis has given way to transports of grief and despair. I'm pretty sure Louis is sweet on Catharine. Mrs. Traill does not mention mosquitoes. I have twenty-seven mosquito bites. I tried sleeping with my sheet over my head but I nearly died of sweating. I am trying self-control not to scratch them. Gladys's are all bleeding. Mother tried putting a baking-soda paste on them but it doesn't really help. The only thing that helps is slapping the bites. But it only helps for a minute. And you have to slap hard.

Dad says mosquitoes like fresh English blood. He says they say to each other, "Fee fi fo fum, I smell the blood of an Englishman."

Question about mosquitoes: Why? I understand about them biting. They want our blood for lunch. But why make an itchy bite? It doesn't do the mosquitoes any good. It makes us more likely to swat them and kill them. And it doesn't do humans any good. Aren't we more likely to get infections if we have bloody wounds on us? It would work out better for everybody if we could just hold out our arms and say, "Come and get it," and give mosquitoes a free lunch without getting itchy.

Mother was at the Homemaker's Club today. The news is that Doctor Johnstone's niece is coming to visit. Her name is Lorayne LaMott and she is seventeen years old and she attends the Marvel School of Cosmetology in Regina.

August 28

A Visitor

Lorayne LaMott has arrived. We were in town shopping and I saw her coming out of the drugstore. She is beautiful. Her hair is perfect. Dark red-brown like Ruby. In little perfect waves. Oh, I wish I could get my hair bobbed. Just looking at her I felt lumpy and mosquito-bite spotty. I wasn't the only one staring either. Wilson Abernathy was staring so hard he tripped over his feet and fell off the boardwalk. I wonder if I'll ever be the type that makes somebody fall over. Or fall in love. Not that I would like Wilson Abernathy to fall for me. He talks through his nose. When Miss Lorayne LaMott walked by the livery stables one of those men who sit outside smoking made a remark. But she just went right on by, with good posture.

August 29

Glamour

Today was a swell day. Miss Lorayne LaMott was in church with Doctor Johnstone and Mrs. Johnstone. After church when all the ladies were chatting Miss LaMott started to talk to Elizabeth and me and then she invited us over for tea. I could tell that Mother was about to say no. (Do parents like saying no?) If she had I would have given way to transports of grief and despair. But when Mrs. Johnstone said please, Mother said yes.

It was lovely. Lorayne (she said we should call her Lorayne) told us that after Cosmetology School she is going to work until she saves enough money to go to Hollywood, California. She wants to be a motion picture actress. After tea she got out her *Photoplay* magazine. Lorayne knows everything about motion pictures. When she found out I was from London she wanted to know what pictures I had seen. I was glad that Auntie Lou had taken us to the pictures. Lorayne knew all about which actors and actresses were in them. I told her about going to the pantomime and she said that many famous movie stars got their start on the stage or in vaudeville. She showed us a picture in *Photoplay* of her favourite actress, Renee Adoree, who got started in the circus. Renee is very pretty. She looks a bit like Lorayne. She was in pictures like *Cape Cod Folks* and *The Big Parade*. Lorayne told us that Renee is under contract with Louis B. Mayer. Under contract is a good thing to be. Lorayne said that movie stars often come from places like Regina or even Milorie and then they get discovered. Then she offered to show us how to put on make-up but Mrs. Johnstone said no, that our mothers would not approve. Then Lorayne said that it didn't matter because we didn't need it because Elizabeth had such smooth skin and I had good bones. "Good bones last," she said. I'm not sure what good bones are but I'm glad I have them. Lorayne said we should come and visit anytime.

On the walk home I decided that Lorayne is like a leghorn and the rest of us are like plain chickens. I know that I have said that Lorayne is like a horse and a chicken but sometimes animals just are prettier than people.

August 30

The Mystery of Goodness

This morning I asked Mother if she didn't think Lorayne was pretty. She made a harrumphing noise and said that she looked like she was no better than she ought to be.

What does that mean? No better than you ought to be isn't bad, is it? Mostly we're all not quite as good as we ought to be. How good ought we to be? We ought to be as good as the Ten Commandments, not coveting or killing or that. But who would be better than that? Only saints I guess, like Florence Nightingale. But then all that means is that Lorayne is not a saint. There was no point in asking Mother. She would just say I was answering back. In this family the eleventh commandment is "Thou shalt not answer back." Besides, whilst thinking about this I let the porridge boil over and Mother said I was sent to try her.

I don't care. I have good bones.

The rest of today was wash day. There is nothing interesting to say about wash day. I'll be happy when school starts.

September 2

News from Overseas

Letter from Ethel today. They went to the seaside for their holidays but it rained every day. Her brother Ronald is getting married! Ethel is going to be a bridesmaid. Lucky. She drew me a picture of Chivers on the back garden wall. I will write back and tell her about Dot. I'll use the Magic Key Line Drawing and draw a picture of Dot's head. (Wouldn't be able to manage legs.)

Ethel sent a joke. Why did the man eat sardines for his tea? So that he would wake up oily in the morning.

I'm going to wake up oily on the first day of school. Four days!!!!

September 3

Lorayne Leaves

BIG SECRET: Today the Homemaker's Club met at our house. Mother spent the morning getting ready and making cakes and a loaf and then after lunch she told us that she didn't want to see hide nor hair of us. William had a day off from the store so he took the twins off to the swimming hole. They've got a rowboat down there now and William is taking some tools and wood down to help fix it. Maybe the boys will be nicer to him when they find out how good he is at carpentry. Maybe that would be as good in stupid boy-thinking as killing gophers.

But I didn't feel like going. So I sneaked back into my room by climbing up onto the roof of the summer kitchen. I thought as long as I was hiding my hide and hair it would be all right. Then I listened down the hole. Here's what I found out. Lorayne has disappeared. And so has Howard Ellingson. Everybody thinks they have gone off together to Regina. But Howard Ellingson has been engaged to Lois Fizzell for two years. They were only waiting until Howard got his own quarter section and then they were going to be married. Mr. and Mrs. Fizzell are furious. Mr. and Mrs. Ellingson are mortified. Mrs. Johnstone is so embarrassed that she didn't even come to the Homemaker's Club. (Although somebody said, "It is not poor Edna Johnstone's fault. How was she to know?") Lois Fizzell is so upset that she has gone to stay with her married sister in Swift Current. Then all the voices said that they weren't surprised, that Lorayne was fast and a flirt and a flapper and no better than she looked. They said that that's what comes of going off to Regina to study cosmetology, that that's what comes of going to too many moving pictures, and that Lois Fizzell was better off without Howard Ellingson because a man who could throw his whole life away on a well-turned ankle was not worth having anyway.

I don't know. I guess it's wrong to steal somebody's fiancée. But it's not like he was kidnapped like Catharine. He must have wanted to go. So why is Lorayne the bad one? Anyway, I want to write this down. I like Miss Lorayne LaMott. I wish she had stayed longer. She is pretty and kind and interesting and she made me feel like somebody. I hope she gets to Hollywood and gets to be in pictures.

September 4

School Barn

The BIG SECRET made me forget about school for one whole day but today I went into town with the Mullers and Elizabeth and I went over to the school. First thing I noticed was a sign on the school barn saying "No Girls Allowed." I asked Elizabeth where the girls stable their horses. She said that girls are allowed to go in the barn before school, for ten minutes at the beginning of lunch hour to feed their horses, and at the end of the day. Otherwise, like at recess, it is boys only.

I asked what was so great about the barn and Elizabeth said did I want to see. So we went in. Big deal! A few stables, lots of manure and a loft full of junk, like pieces of tin, old boards, tops of desks. Why would the boys want to spend time here anyway? It smells dreadful.

We looked in the windows of the school. It is just one room. There are rows of desks for two and blackboards on three walls.

In the schoolyard there are some swings.

I can't wait till school starts.

September 6

A Happy End to Adversity
(I stole this from Mrs. Traill)

I finished *Lost in the Backwoods*. Catharine was rescued. After three years they all get home safely. Later on Catharine and Louis get married. It seems to me that she is going to find it a bit dull, cooking breakfast and washing nappies.

September 7

First Day of School

Finally! I've been wondering about school ever since we came to Canada. The best thing was riding Dot. As we were riding along the road I thought of Ethel starting the term at Sandringham

Road School and I wished that she was sitting on a fence along the road looking at me go by. Ivy Weatherall, barefoot Canadian farm girl, riding a horse to school! Second-best thing was our teacher, Miss Hutchinson. She's lovely. She has bobbed hair, very clean fingernails and a soft voice. She welcomed "our English newcomers." Gladys and Harry were a bit scared because it is their very first day of school and Miss Hutchinson was kind and jokey with them.

Here is what the school is like. When you go in there is a porch with a shelf to put your lunch pail. If you forget and leave it on the floor gophers come in and steal your lunch. Elizabeth told me that last year people's lunches started disappearing and everyone was blaming everyone else. It turned out that the little boy who lives across the street was wandering in and helping himself to the nicest things.

In Canada they have grades, not forms, and I am in grade six. The other grade sixes are Elizabeth, Klaus Berg, Toffee-Nose and the home-run boy with the pig, Abel Butt. I get to sit with Elizabeth. Harry and Gladys sit together. Gladys didn't know that she was supposed to stay at her desk so she kept coming over to sit with me. When Miss Hutchinson said she had to stay at her desk she cried so Miss H. said she could sit with me just for one day. By lunchtime she was feeling happy.

She stood on her head in the schoolyard and her knickers showed.

At the front of the classroom is the teacher's desk on a little stage. Today there was a jam jar with flowers. Miss H. decorated the tops of the blackboards with birds and flowers in coloured chalk. She is a good artist.

At the back there is a black stove and at the side is a bench with a pail of water and a tin cup.

We started off with the Lord's Prayer, just like home. Then we sang "The Maple Leaf Forever," which is different. Then we got our readers and rearranged the desks.

We didn't do much work. We got our new scribblers. Mine is called a Red Monarch and it has a lovely picture of a lion on the front. On the back it has weights and measures. This is useful because I can never remember all that about pecks and bushels and rods and furlongs and miles. This year I am going to be very neat.

The grade eight boys, Lars Hansen, Ralph Battrum, and Hans started to act like they knew it all and were making noise and answering back and then Miss Hutchinson did something very remarkable. She took the strap out of her desk. We were shocked. We thought she was going to strap them. But instead she threw it in the stove and said, "If anybody disrupts the class so that we cannot learn, what will happen to them will make them wish I had kept the strap." Well! That made even Lars, Ralph and Hans be quiet as mice.

September 8

Mistake

I've cooked my goose with Toffee-Nose. And I didn't even mean to. Today she was talking about how she had been to Regina to visit her older sister and they had been to the cinema. She told us that she had seen a picture called *The Pilgrim* with Charlie Chaplin. And I jumped in without thinking and said that I had seen it too and wasn't it funny when Charlie Chaplin pours pudding sauce all over that man's hat? Toffee-Nose got very quiet and said that I couldn't have seen it because it had just come to Regina. So then I said that I had seen it in London before we came here. Then she said that I must be lying. Then she said that there wasn't any bit with pudding sauce. Which is a real lie. What a sneak! So I said that there certainly was and I described in detail all about the hat and why Charlie Chaplin, who is a crook disguised as a minister, thinks it is a pudding and how he put whipped cream and decorations on as well. Then she just flounced away. Who cares? Good riddance. All day she kept giving me cold looks and at the lunch hour she had her lunch with Florence Gilmour and Nellie

McLaren and she looked over at me and said something and laughed. Then they all laughed. I ate with Elizabeth and the twins.

Here is the important thing that I forgot: Never take attention away from a show-off. This is true in England and Canada.

September 9

School Barn Secrets Revealed

I found out a bit of what goes on in the school barn. Today Ralph came in from recess with an eye full of tomato seeds. The junk in the loft of the barn isn't just junk. It is forts, one at each end. And there are two gangs. At recess the gangs have battles. They take their slingshots and they attack each other with rabbit droppings and pieces of mud and, today, tomatoes. Ralph was hiding behind a desk top and looking out the inkwell hole and a tomato got him right in the eye. Miss Hutchinson washed it out with two cups of water. Nyla looked down her toffee nose at the boys and said they were barbarians. But, secret: I would like a slingshot. I know they are not lady-like. I'll bet Catharine could use a slingshot if she needed to.

September 11

Flies Are Not My Friends

I'm not so keen on milking anymore. There are a lot of flies and they land all over me. Flies can make me very annoyed. They torment Daisy and she uses her tail to shoo them away. But then her tail slaps me on the back of the head.

September 14

How Long Is Canada?

Today Miss Hutchinson said that as a special treat all the grade sevens and eights could come in and out the windows instead of using the door. Harry is fit to burst with envy. He asked me how long it is till grade seven. I told him six years. He said, "Is that as long as Canada?"

It was very hot in school today. Everybody was going over to the water bucket every other minute. The school smells like varnish.

September 15

An Enemy

Somebody doesn't like us. On the way to school there is a place by the side of the road that is sandy. This morning somebody had written "Brit-ishers Go Home" in the sand. I stopped Dot dead in her tracks. I was surprised and then really cross. I got off Dot and rubbed it out. The twins wanted to know what it said. I told them it was nothing. Which it is. Just words. All the same it gave me a funny stomachache feeling all day.

September 16

The Enemy Continues

It was there again this morning. But bigger. I rubbed it out again.

Who?

Why?

September 17

Enemy Identified

The sand writer strikes again. This morning whilst I was rubbing out the insult Elizabeth and the boys came by in their wagon. I told them what was up. Elizabeth says it is obviously Nyla. The clues are that she comes in on this road, she gets to school early and she is a sneaky, mean person. Then Hans said that she is the sort of person who would use the word "Britisher." They think we should reply. Harry thought this was a great idea. He had a suggestion right away but it was very rude. I don't care to write that word in my diary. Where did Harry learn it? Has he been going in the school barn at recess?

We're all going to think about it until tomorrow.

September 20

Revenge

We did it. It was Gladys who thought of it. Elizabeth and Hans think Gladys is brilliant. She is. This morning we left for school early. When we got to the right place we wrote, "N.M. is a Congenital Psychopathic Inferior Person. Signed: The Britishers (and friends)," in the sand.

Nyla gave me some black looks today but I just smiled back in a cheery way.

September 22

This is a quiz:

Who likes puddles?

1. Ducks? (correct)
2. Makers of galoshes? (correct)
3. The twins? (correct)
4. Dot? (extra correct)

Last night it rained. There were puddles all over the road. Dot walked around them carefully and then just before we got to school there was a huge one that went all across the road. All of a sudden Dot just lay down. The twins and I had to jump off in a big hurry before she rolled right on top of us.

But we ended up in the puddle anyway. We were covered in mud. Harry even had mud in his eyebrows. Everything went flying. Our books, our lunch pails, Dot's food. She just rolled in the mud looking happy, happy, happy. Then she stood up, gave a shake and looked around at us as though she was saying, "Time to go."

But there was no fence to climb up so we couldn't get back on. Besides we didn't want to get up on her muddy back. So we walked the rest of the way, leading Dot.

When we got to school Miss Hutchinson said we should sit outside until we dried. Then she brushed us off. At recess I cleaned Dot.

Good thing about mud puddles: There was no message in the sand today.

September 26

How to Be a Saint

Today in church Mr. Quigley gave a sermon about saints. He said that anybody can be a saint. You don't have to be a fisherman in sandals or burnt in a fire or sit on a pole for twenty years or stuff like that. You can be a saint by being patient or generous or turning the other cheek. But I don't think I'm going to try to be a saint. It's hard enough to be good in the regular way.

September 27

Poor William

Dad and William are away. They both have jobs on a threshing rig in some town called Stanton. Mr. Burgess is managing without William because he knows that threshing is a well-paid job.

I wish I could get a job. Dad said that when we came to Canada there would be lots of proper jobs but so far it is just like home with a bit of this and that. Dad has been a farm worker, a blacksmith's helper, a grain elevator cleaner and a railway track repairman. Mother has been an egg lady. Mr. Burgess has been very kind to us but William is the only one with a proper job. Hope we don't end up like Uncle Alf, owing money and living in a dirt house.

If we were at home William would be out playing conkers with his school friends on Halley Road. Here he is working like a grown-up man. This makes me feel a bit sad, as though he is a stranger.

September 28

A Hero

Hans wasn't in school today because he is working on the harvest. Ralph Battrum and Lars Hansen were away too.

In my reader today I read all about Edith Cavell, who was a heroic nurse in the Great War. She cared for all the suffering and wounded soldiers and then she helped some Belgian soldiers escape from the Germans. The Germans found out and they put her in prison and then they shot her. She was a "noble character." I think she sounds like a saint.

September 30

The Reader

First month of school and Gladys has already read everything in the primer. Miss Hutchinson says she can go on to the *Canadian Reader Book One*.

October 1

Thunder and Kindness

Today was very hot, like being under a pile of blankets. At recess we were all playing anti-I-over across the school roof when all of a sudden, out of nowhere, there was a huge crash of thunder. The ground shivered. I looked over at the swings where Harry was waiting for his turn and he was crouched on the ground with his hands over his ears and his eyes squeezed shut. I started over to talk to him when Miss Hutchinson picked him up and took him inside. When we came in from recess Miss Hutchinson was cuddling Harry on her lap.

His eyes were still shut. On the blackboard was written. "Go on with your work. Nobody is to tease Harry about this."

Miss Hutchinson is a very kind person.

Harry likes to hear about bombs and such. He loves William's stories about hiding in the cellar during the bombing raids in London. But he hates loud noises in real life. I think he had better give up his plan to be an anarchist. He's not going to be very good at blowing things up.

October 2

Harvest

Today I went over to Elizabeth's to help take doughnuts to the harvesters.

The harvesters have their breakfast (bacon, sausages, eggs, pancakes, toast, jam and apple pie) at five o'clock, so by nine o'clock they need more food. Mrs. Muller's doughnuts are delicious. No, delicious isn't the right word. It is too little. They are manna. Last Sunday in church, Mr. Quigley read the lesson about the children of Israel lost in the wilderness and how God sent them manna in the morning. Mr. Quigley said that the Bible said that manna was like wafers made with honey and we should think of the most delicious thing we could. I thought of Mrs. Muller's doughnuts. She piles those doughnuts into big baskets lined with napkins and Elizabeth and I take them out to the fields. Then when we come back Mrs. Muller gives us little round doughnut holes.

Then we went out to watch the threshing machine. It is a wonder. It looks like a hungry animal gobbling the sheaves of grain. You can watch it for hours without getting bored. Gears and wheels and belts and big knives and a big steam engine. Grain spilling into the granary and straw blowing out a pipe and making a big pile. Mr. Muller walks around oiling and greasing and adjusting bits of machinery. It is the first time I've seen him smile.

P.S. One more thing about doughnuts and manna. The best part of the Bible story is how the children of Israel aren't allowed to save any of their manna for the next day. If they try it the manna gets worms in it and goes all nasty. Mrs. Muller wouldn't need to worry about that. There would be no chance of finding worms in the doughnuts the next day because the harvesters never leave ANY LEFTOVERS.

October 3

Harvest Done

The harvest is over and I think there is going to be trouble at Elizabeth's house. Today just as we were getting ready to take out the doughnuts all the men arrived home. Nine o'clock in the morning and the harvest was done! Mrs. Muller took a kitchen chair out to the yard and put a basin of water on it, and a towel over the back and the men took off their shirts. When they take off their shirts it is like they still have pale shirts on, with brown necks and arms and the rest white. They started washing and spraying drops of water over the yard and running water through their hair. All those drops of water just lay in the dust, not sinking in. The men ate doughnuts and drank coffee and larked about, whooping, and carrying on like it was the last day of school. One of the harvesters juggled doughnuts and another one walked on his hands. Mr. Muller didn't fool about though. He didn't eat doughnuts either. He's like that thin man in Mother Goose: "Jack Spratt would eat no fat."

But then Gerhard threw his hat way up into the tree. All the men laughed and one said, "How are you going to get your hat down?" There was a long silence and then Gerhard said, "I don't need to get it down. I don't need that hat. That's it. I got in this harvest and now I'm never going to farm one more minute in my entire life." The words just sat there like drops of water in the dust. Gerhard didn't sound angry, just very clear. I saw Hans and Elizabeth all sneak looks at their father. I did too. He looked like his face was made of rock. And he just turned and went into the house. Gerhard went back to his doughnut. I wonder what will happen. Elizabeth will tell me.

October 4

Harvesters Home

Dad and William are home. Tonight at supper they told us all about threshing. Dad drove the rack and team. William was a spike pitcher. That is the person who loads bundles with the pitchfork. He said that after his first day he was so weary that he couldn't even eat his supper. The farm family was so sorry for him that they let him sleep in their spare bedroom, rather than in the granary on a cot with the rest of the crew. But it wasn't much of a favour because the bed had bedbugs and he didn't sleep a wink! But after that things got easier and he loved the food.

Later, when we were alone, William told me that a man on their crew got his hand caught in the machinery and lost two fingers. William is blinking a lot again.

October 5

A Package from Eaton's

My long underwear arrived. Two pairs. They are scratchy and they make me look lumpy. Mother says I have to wear them even though it is hardly cold at all. I'm sure that Renee Adoree never had to wear long underwear.

October 6

News from the Mullers

Gerhard is gone. Elizabeth says he was very cheerful and helpful for a few days and this morning he was gone. He left a note saying he was going to Calgary and that they were not to worry. Elizabeth says her father read the note out loud and then he crumpled it up and threw it in the stove. Then he said they were not to mention Gerhard again. Elizabeth said that Gerhard didn't even say goodbye to her.

I feel sorry for Elizabeth with such a stern father. If William ran away from home (maybe you can't call it running away when someone is sixteen, like Gerhard) Dad would never say he wouldn't talk about him.

Elizabeth was very quiet in school today. She's biting her nails again. Herman was so naughty that Miss Hutchinson made him stand in a corner. And Hans didn't come to school.

I wonder if Gerhard said goodbye to Worm-Emily Piggott?

October 9

The Truth About Long Underwear

It stretches. Every day the legs get longer and longer. After the third day you have to roll them up. By Friday — elephant legs!

October 10

Marrow Memories

Harvest Festival at church today. The flowers and fruit made it look just like St. Edmund's at home. I must have started thinking about home because there were big squashes on the altar steps and whilst the sermon was on I remembered the time Ethel and I wrote rude words with pins on her father's baby vegetable marrows. The marrows grew and grew and the rude words grew and grew. Nobody knew who had done it. I almost started to laugh so I had to pretend I was coughing. Why does church make me get the giggles?

October 12

Worry

Dot is sick. When I went to get her from the barn after school she was lying down and she wouldn't get up. I didn't know what to do but Miss Hutchinson said I should go to the livery stable and get Mr. Battrum. He said that it was likely colic and he came over to the school with some ginger and turpentine. But Dot still didn't get up. Mr. Battrum said it would take a while and we should just walk home. He said he would keep an eye on Dot until tomorrow. It was a long sad walk home. Harry held my hand and tried to cheer me up by saying riddles. I wish I could have stayed with Dot. I love her.

October 13

Worry Over

Dot is right as rain. She was very happy to see me. I gave her extra oats.

October 15

Horrible News

Children are slaves. Children don't have any say and they just get pushed around. It is NOT FAIR.

At tea Dad announced that we're moving to town. Since one of the banks closed down there is an extra building and we're going to rent it and live there and run it as a hotel. He also said that it will be much easier for us to get to school in winter and for William to get to the store. Also, Mr. Battrum has offered Dad work at the livery stables.

This whole idea is silly. The argument about school is silly. It will be no problem getting to school from the farm. We don't need to move into town for that. If we can't ride Dot we can hitch her to a sleigh. I could drive a sleigh. Hans and Elizabeth do. Elizabeth told me all about it. They have hot hard-boiled eggs to keep their hands warm and then they eat the eggs for lunch. It is perfectly fine. I want to drive a sleigh. William could come in the sleigh to work.

The VERY WORST THING is that we have to give Dot back to Mr. Burgess. Why don't I get a say? Women have the vote, but not children. I told Mother and Dad that our family was not a democracy. And they laughed! I am cross as hops. I am going out to the barn to visit Dot and if they think I'm going to do any chores tonight they are wrong. Chores can go hang.

October 16

Barn Thoughts

I'm in the barn. Dad and William have gone to town. Dad asked me if I wanted to come. But I said no thank you. I also said no thank you to breakfast. I am treating them with cold disdain.

Mother is in the kitchen ordering things like sheets and celery dishes from the catalogue, for when we have the hotel. This is daft. Why don't they just take the money they're going to spend on that stuff and use it so we can stay on the farm?

My days with Dot are numbered so I'm just going to go for a ride. Maybe I won't come back. If Mother needs me to mind the twins or anything I just won't be here. She hasn't said anything about me not doing the chickens.

What about the egg money? We won't have that when we're in town. That's what I should have said.

Later

It didn't work. I took Dot out for a ride and she wouldn't go any direction except toward school. When I tried to make her go the other way she just stood there, completely still. So much for escaping.

Tonight is bath night. Mother is heating the water right now. I would like to refuse with cold disdain. I would like to say, "I don't want to share water with traitors." But I don't think I'll be able to manage it. I like bath night too much.

October 17

Visit to the Prison

Today we went to see the bank-hotel-house. Mother was full of plans. She went on and on about how lovely the floor is. Who cares about floors when you have to give your horse away? The bank part is going to be the parlour and sitting room for the guests. In the back and upstairs is like a normal house. The kitchen has a trapdoor that leads down into the cellar by a ladder. This is the only thing that is one bit interesting.

Daisy will go back to the Mullers. How can Mother do this?

October 18

Dull Day

Packing, cleaning, sorting, packing, cleaning, sorting.

Dull to do. Dull to write about.

It's Halley Road all over again. Today the chickens went. Some farmer came and took them. I did collect the eggs this morning because I knew it would be the last time. Chicken pecked me as usual.

I'm trying to remember every step of riding Dot to school.

Today we had a grammar bee. I did not excel. Grammar is just as confusing in Canada as it was in England. I know when to say *me* and *I* and all that. Mother is very stern about that kind of grammar. But I just can't do parsing. I can't remember what parts of the sentence are called. What does it matter if something is an adverb clause? I guess it matters to Klaus Berg. He won, and his family doesn't even speak English at home.

The only good thing about today was that I wore the new frock that Mother made me out of one of her old ones. But then even that was spoiled. Nyla looked at it, looking down her nose the way she does, and said, "That's an interesting style. Did it come from the Eaton's catalogue?" I said no, that Mother made it and she said, "Oh," (little pause), "homemade." She makes me cross enough to spit. Of course she knew it was homemade. I fell for it. I should have just said, "No, Nyla," and left her hanging.

October 19

Black Tuesday

Dot has gone. I'm too sad to write.

October 21

I don't know what to do. I'm in the farmhouse alone with the twins. Today is moving day and Mother and Dad and William have gone to town with the first load of furniture. They borrowed a team of horses and a hay rack to move us. But they haven't come back and it is snowing hard.

At first it was fun being in the house alone. We

played hide and seek and yelled a lot. We ate bread and molasses for lunch and didn't use table manners. Then we played cross-channel ferry which is where you put a twin in the wash tub and push it around the floor.

But after lunch it got very dark and we looked out and it was snowing. So we all ran outside. Our first snow! We ran around and tried to catch it on our tongues. I remember snow once at home but the twins don't remember it at all. Harry wanted to build an igloo right away but there wasn't enough snow and it wasn't sticky. Then we were all cold and the snow had turned into needles. So we came in. And the fire was nearly out. I put more coal in and we ate more bread and molasses. Then we told stories. I told them *The Three Pigs* and *The Three Bears* and a made-up story about chickens. Then Harry told a story about the bogeyman and the bogeywife and the bogeyhouse and the bogeybaby who went around in a bogeypram. It was very silly but Gladys loved it. They seem happy enough. But now it is getting dark and Mother and Dad are not back. Where are they?

Later

I just put the last piece of coal in the stove. The fire is eating it up very fast. I found some candles. You can't see anything out the windows except snow blowing in the darkness. The little ones are hungry but they don't want more bread and molasses which is the only thing we have. I want Mother and Dad to come right now. Before I finish writing this extra-long-waiting-to-hear-them sentence I want to hear them in the yard. Before I finish writing this long sentence I want to hear the horses. Can horses walk in snow? What if they all got caught in the snow? They are not here. What would Louis and Hector and Catharine do? I'm trying to remember the book.

Even Later

Why doesn't somebody come? I don't know what time it is. I found some rugs and wrapped up the twins in front of the stove. There isn't any more coal. I'm burning the meadow muffins that I collected last summer. But there aren't many more. If only I could go to town and get help. But how? When they left Dad said, "Take care of the little ones." I'm trying. I don't want to have to be the grown-up.

I'm looking at the kitchen chairs and I don't see chairs. I see wood. There used to be a hatchet propped just outside the door, unless they took it.

October 22

The Story of Yesterday

Yesterday was the most frightening day of my life. After I finished writing that about the chairs I decided I did have to chop them up for the stove. I could feel the cold creeping down the walls and Harry was crying. But I couldn't open the door to look for the hatchet because snow was drifted against it. So I broke the kitchen window and crawled out and felt around in the snow and I did find the hatchet. I tried to wedge the washtub into the broken window with some rags but it didn't work very well.

It is harder to chop up chairs than it looks. And all the time I was wondering if I was going to get into the biggest trouble ever. But I did it. First the six kitchen chairs and then, when they were burnt up, Mother's rocking chair that she brought from England. The twins just stared at me. Then I think I must have gone to sleep because I woke up to Dad and Mr. Burgess coming in the door. The snow had stopped. They came in a sleigh. Dad hugged us all together and cried. He said he got trapped in town in the blizzard. He said that chopping up the chairs was a very sensible thing to do and that he was proud of me and that I was becoming very Canadian. Then they wrapped us all in rugs and took us to town and Mother hugged us and cried too. Even William got wet eyes.

I'm very tired.

October 23

First Day in the Hotel

Everything is higgledy piggledy but Mother let me lie in anyway. She brought me tea and porridge in bed just like I was sick. The sun has come out and there is a sound of dripping outside the windows. The twins are roaring around in some room or other. I need to get up and explore the Weatherall Hotel.

Evening

Dad brought home the *Milorie Messenger* to show us the advertisement for the hotel. It says:

> First-Class Rooms and Board
> Mrs. S. Weatherall
> Bank Building
> Milorie, Sask.

Harry asked what does "first-class" mean and Dad said it means celery dishes. And then Mother rapped him on the head with her knuckles.

October 24

The blizzard is like a bad dream.

October 25

Coming Event

Hallowe'en! Today Miss Hutchinson said that our seatwork was cutting ghosts out of white paper for Hallowe'en. But I didn't know what Hallowe'en (I like the way that word looks, with the little apostrophe between the e's) was, so Miss H. said who will tell Ivy about Hallowe'en. And everyone started in, like the Tower of Babel. They told me about dressing up and jack-o'-lanterns, stealing pumpkins, bobbing for apples, hiding in the chicken coop, saying "apples or tricks." It is the best Canadian thing. (No, I take it back. Not as good as Dot and doughnuts but almost as good.) Abel was just starting to tell me about what tricks to play on people when Miss H. made us all be quiet.

None of those Canada books we got in London said one thing about Hallowe'en. If they want new settlers to come to Canada they should mention Hallowe'en. Then all the children would make their parents come. Kids should write those books. Grown-ups don't know what's important.

October 26

The Monster

Elizabeth told me about a really scary thing that happened to her last Hallowe'en. Scary, then funny.

There was going to be a party at the school on the night before Hallowe'en. She and Hans were walking to it. They were getting themselves scared for the fun of it, talking about ghouls and walking spirits and all that. And they passed by our house (I mean our old house — the Fretwell house), but nobody lived there then. Elizabeth thought she heard singing coming from the dark house so they went over to investigate. And they just got up to the door and it swung open and there was a monster standing there. It had a tiger's head, a monkey's tail and three horns. So they took off like crazy down the road, running as fast as they could. And they could hear the monster running behind them. Then Elizabeth tripped and fell. She said that all she could think of was that the monster was going to gore her to death with his horns. But then she heard this noise and the monster was standing over her laughing. And she looked up and there was Florence Gilmour's older brother Tom holding a mask. Turns out he was on his way to the party and he stopped at the empty house to put on his costume because he didn't want anyone to see it in advance. He was humming some old song to himself — that was the sound they heard. He said that he was calling "Stop, Elizabeth," and "Hans, it's only me." But Elizabeth could only hear her own breathing and her heart thumping. They all had a good laugh.

October 28

Time Stands Still

This is worse than waiting for my birthday. Mother said that Hallowe'en sounds like an excuse for a bunch of hooligans, and give her Guy Fawkes Day any day. But she did find me some old raggedy clothes. I've decided to dress up like a tramp. Elizabeth is going to go as an old Granny.

Today at recess Nyla came up to me with a nicey nicey look on her face and said she was sorry that we had to live in a boarding house. I told her it was not a boarding house but a first-class hotel. "Oh yes?" she said in that perfectly poisonous way.

I'll bet the Muirs don't have celery dishes. That's what I should have said.

October 29

Intrigue

Today Elizabeth passed me a note. It said, "Secret message. Meet me by the stump at lunch." I meet Elizabeth for lunch every day anyway. But I like getting notes even though if Miss Hutchinson catches us she gives us lines. The secret is that Elizabeth overheard Hans and Ralph planning to scare us on Hallowe'en. They know we're going to be at the Mullers' getting our costumes ready. They are going to get Mrs. Muller to ask us to go to the chicken house just around dusk and they are going to be hiding in there in ghost costumes to scare us. Over lunch we planned our counter-attack. It is an excellent plan.

November 1

What Really Happened on Hallowe'en

This might be short. I'm so sleepy. We were up until 10:30 last night. Miss Hutchinson said we were all dopes in school. But Hallowe'en was crackerjack. We locked the boys in the chicken house and we pretended we couldn't hear them shouting. We just said things like, "My, aren't the chickens noisy tonight," and "Good thing the chickens are safe because you never know what might happen on Hallowe'en." We let them out after about ten minutes when we got them to say that we were lovely, kind and beautiful.

Then we all went into town and did "apples and tricks" at people's houses. Almost everybody gave us an apple except for old Mr. Olson who didn't even open his door. Hans said we should overturn his outhouse so we snuck around to the back but just when we got up to it he jumped out of it and came after us with a broom. So we escaped and we didn't get to play any tricks. But we got lots of apples. All over the streets there were clowns, and hunters, witches, more tramps, ghosts. Abel was a jailbird. Nyla was a gypsy with gold ear hoops and a red sateen skirt with flounces. Her mother sewed her a costume. It is nicer than most people's real clothes. But she had to go home for ordinary bedtime. We got to stay up late. It was like kids owned Milorie. This morning I heard that Mr. Skidmore set up a booby trap for the next outhouse tippers. They were supposed to fall down the hole. But it backfired and *he* did! Cannot write one more thing except that I would like to dress like a tramp all the time. You can do anything and not worry about getting dirty.

November 2

Outhouses vs Door Knockers

Today I heard about a few more tricks that happened on Hallowe'en, like the cream separator that ended up on the roof of the school, and whose screen door got soaped. Which is a better place for playing tricks, England or Canada? Canada is good because of Hallowe'en and outhouses. But there is one English trick that you can't play here because the houses are too far apart. It is called knocking on doors. Here's how you do it: You take a piece of string and you tie it to the door knocker of one house. Then you tie the other end to the door knocker of the house next door. You have to tie it nice and tight. Then you knock on door number one and you hide. The person in house number one answers their door, doesn't see anybody and closes their door. This makes the string knock on door number two. The person in house number two opens their door, looks, closes their door. This makes the knocker knock on door number one. And so it goes on back and forth. The record on Halley Road, which was by Peggy Plumley, was twelve times. (You can play knocking on doors any time of the year. That's another good thing about it. Point for England.)

November 5

War

Today Miss Hutchinson talked about Armistice Day which is next Monday. She talked about the Great War and said we should be grateful for all the men and women who gave up their lives so that there would never be another war. I thought of Edith Cavell. Then I thought of Dad's brother, Uncle Ted. He was killed at the Battle of the Somme, but when William was an infant he met him. Then Miss Hutchinson read "In Flanders Fields." She told us that the poem was written by a Canadian doctor and that the next battles we all had to fight were the battles against disease.

At recess the boys played enemy attack. Boys are loathsome.

When I got home only Dad was there. He was reading the paper. "Glorious dead," he said. Then he hit it with the back of his hand and said that there wasn't that much glorious about it and all the politicians were silly asses here, just like in England. Then he said that the only man that could really run the country would be a woman. Take Queen Victoria! Take your mother! She'd keep them all in line, she would. She'd be a dandy prime minister.

Then he said bundle up and let's go for a walk. So we did.

I told Dad that I had been thinking about Uncle Ted. He told me how Uncle Ted was so clever that he made his own bicycle. Dad told me about a mate of his in Gibraltar, too.

Then he said how when he came home from the war he had a beard and William didn't know his own father and cried when he picked him up. He said that after the war the toffs came home and took up their lives again but there was nothing for the ordinary working man. No jobs even though they had been promised them. He said, "You're a hero when you're over there, but nobody wants to know about you when you come home."

Then he got very quiet and sad. But just for a little while. Then he said it was all ancient history and why didn't we have a song and he sang "On the Road to Mandalay." This is a very good song to sing LOUD, especially the "dawn comes up like thunder" bit. We really let rip.

P.S. If we were home, today would be Guy Fawkes Day. Harry is sad that they don't do Guy Fawkes Day in Canada because he loves Guy Fawkes because he was going to blow up the Houses of Parliament. I don't care though. I like Hallowe'en better.

November 7

Incident with a Pie

Mother made pumpkin pies to celebrate our first Canadian Thanksgiving. She got the recipe from the Homemaker's Club. Pies from squash sounds horrid but it turns out to be scrumptious. But I had an accident with one. I was in the kitchen showing Harry how I can do a front flip, but it wasn't a perfect front flip and at the end I had to grab the counter and I put my hand right into one of the pies. Harry was very pleased. He liked the accident better than the flip. But Mother came in before I could repair the pie. She said what was she going to do with me. So one pie was a bit scrambled. But it tasted dandy.

November 10

Bed and Board

Finally everything in the hotel is shipshape and we have our first guest. He's not a traveller. His name is Mr. Ambrose. He is quite old. His wife died two years ago. His children are grown up and live far away. When he came to look at the room he told Mother that he felt he was in danger of falling into bachelor ways, such as living on beans. Mr. Ambrose is very polite. He also said he would enjoy some stimulating conversation with others from the old country. I wonder how stimulating he will find it when the twins start speaking their secret language. He will have the front room. Mother's advertisement said, "Favourable terms for long-term guests," which means he pays less than travelling salesmen would pay. He moves in on Thursday.

November 11

Moving Day

Mr. Ambrose moved in today. William says he had some very heavy boxes. Mother has laid down the law that we are not to talk his ear off.

November 12

Extinction

Mystery solved. The heavy boxes were an encyclopedia. Today when I came home after school Mr. Ambrose was in the sitting room reading this fat leather book. He started to tell me about this huge flightless bird called the great auk. I knew he liked stimulating conversation so I asked what happened to the auk and he told me about extinction. Then he told me that since he stopped farming he has started to read the encyclopedia, because he didn't have much chance of an education when he was a lad and it is never too late. Then he said that it would be a great favour to him if I would think of a question every day to ask him.

November 15

Sea Story

Question of the day: Why are there seagulls flying over the fields around Milorie when we are so far from the sea in both directions? When I asked Mr. Ambrose he looked as though I had offered him a sweet. He brought several volumes of the encyclopedia down to the sitting room and started leafing and reading. We didn't really find the answer but along the way he told me that long long ago the prairies were under the sea. I said how did we know and he got even happier and said was I free to go for a walk. Then he went into the kitchen and asked Mother if he could borrow me for an hour for a scientific expedition. I knew there were dishes to wash and twins to mind but Mother said yes. (I like having boarders!)

We walked out the main road toward the Muller farm and Mr. Ambrose talked about the Cretaceous Epoch, before the Rocky Mountains, when dinosaurs walked the earth. Then we took off down a little track and came to a low sandy bit of land. Mr. Ambrose crouched down and began running the sand through his fingers and then he pulled out a little bit of broken rock with a swirly pattern in it, about the size of my little fingernail. He said it was the fossil of a sea snail that had lived right here, when here was a shallow sea, a hundred million years ago. Then he found something that might have been a bit of squid. He gave them to me. I'm going to collect fossils. That would be a good collection for a deep-sea diver.

On the walk home I thought about a hundred million years. I thought about a hundred million diaries. In my head I flew up high, like a seagull, and looked down at Mr. Ambrose and me and we looked like tiny ants crawling across the world. We were quiet on the way home and didn't have stimulating conversation but Mr. Ambrose didn't seem to mind.

November 16

Jazz Man

The Mullers finally had a letter from Gerhard. He has joined a jazz band and he's travelling all over. He's playing the trumpet. Gerhard never even had a trumpet. Elizabeth says he used to go over to the Elliots' place and play Mel Elliot's dad's bugle that he brought home from the war. (Mel Elliot's dad brought it back, not Gerhard. Miss Hutchinson says that this is an ambiguous pronoun reference and she has many amusing examples of it, but I don't think it matters because obviously Gerhard didn't bring home a bugle from the war, he was only a baby.) Anyway, he must have got good enough at the trumpet to be in a band. In his letter he said that he played in a new dance hall in Manitou Beach that has a dance floor that has horsehair under it. The horsehair makes it very bouncy for dancers.

I don't understand. Back home Grandma had a horsehair sofa and it wasn't bouncy at all. It was as hard as a rock. You got numb sitting on it. And when I touched Dot's mane and tail it wasn't bouncy. To be really bouncy wouldn't the dance floor have to be on rubber? That would be a good question for Mr. Ambrose.

Mr. Muller is still so angry at Gerhard that he wouldn't even read the letter.

November 17

Magic Words

Snow. Not a blizzard, but big white flakes. It started this morning just after we went in to school. Everybody was looking out the windows and not paying attention. Finally Miss Hutchinson said we could have early recess. Everybody practically fell over each other getting on their mitts and scarves. Harry was disappointed because it still isn't the kind of snow you can pack into snowballs or igloos. But he cheered up when everyone started playing fox and geese. For this game you tramp out the pattern of a wagon wheel in the snow. It is sort of like tag. The fox is It and everyone else is a goose. But you have to stay on the lines of the wheel and the spokes. If you have to pass someone mostly you fall over in the snow and then you're out. Miss Hutchinson played with us and she let us have double recess. I had to pass Nyla and she fell over and then she got very huffy and dropped out of the game. She gave me a nasty look, which is ridiculous.

When we came back in everyone was soaking so Miss Hutchinson let us sit around the stove and she read to us instead of doing our lessons. She made us promise to work extra hard tomorrow. The story she read was *Ali Baba and the Forty Thieves.*

All the boys liked this story because of the gruesome deaths, like being drowned in boiling oil.

I liked the part where the greedy brother forgets the magic words Open Sesame and starts saying things like Open Barley. That is exactly what would happen to me. I'd forget the magic words. There I would be, Ivy Weatherall stuck in a cave. I would heard the bloodthirsty robbers coming. Open Wheat! I would hear their horses. Open Rye! I would hear the crash of their cruel weapons. Open Oatmeal! Trapped!

This is what I was thinking about when I wasn't doing my dictionary drill.

(True confession: I did give Nyla a bit of a shove in fox and geese. I just couldn't resist.)

November 20

Music through the Air

This evening the Mullers invited us over to listen to their new tube radio. Hans came and got us in the sleigh. The runners on the sleigh make a beautiful sound on the snow. I felt like the Snow Queen in the fairy tale.

The radio is a Westinghouse two-tube. It is super. Much better than the crystal wireless that Dad had on Halley Road. He used to fiddle with it all the time trying to get something. Mother said she was going to chuck it in the dustbin if he didn't stop wasting time. The tube radio is much better. It gets stations from as far away as other provinces, like Edmonton, Alberta, and even from other countries, like Salt Lake City, U.S.A. It has two sets of earphones so we took turns.

Mr. Muller kept twisting the dials to find different places. Mother and Dad listened to a man from Regina giving a talk on growing vegetables. It was torture to wait for our turn. William and I were next and Mr. Muller found us a lady in Toronto singing. I shut my eyes and it was like having a soprano singing inside my head. But she started fading away and then there was a sound like frying so Mr. Muller twisted the dials again and found a little kids' show. It was "Good Night Stories with Mr. Radiobug." So we gave the headphones to the twins. It was comical to see them laughing at the same time when we didn't even know what they were listening to.

When it was over Harry asked how the stories got into the box. Hans explained about radio waves and that. I don't really understand it.

Mrs. Muller made tea and then Elizabeth and I shared one pair of headphones and Hans took the other. He found some wonderful music. It was horns and a banjo and drums and I couldn't tell what else. But you couldn't listen to it without starting to move around. So we were jigging around and Elizabeth started snapping her fingers and Mr. Muller took the headphones off Hans and listened and then switched off the radio. In an angry way. He said that it was jazz and that jazz is wicked music. Probably because of Gerhard running away to join a jazz band.

On the way home Harry kept throwing his hands up in the air. Dad asked him what he was doing and he said that he was trying to feel the radio waves. Everybody laughed but, truth to tell, I wonder about that too. If they are going right through me on their way from CKCK Regina to the Mullers' radio, wouldn't I feel them? I certainly hope we get a radio when our ship comes in.

November 21

Question of the Day

My question for Mr. Ambrose today was, can music be wicked? He said that was going to take a lot of reading and thinking.

November 22

Chocolate Bomb

Today one of the little boys, Thorvald Berg, who is in grade one, put his tin pail of cocoa on the stove at school to heat up and he forgot to take the lid off a bit. In the middle of the grade six spelling drill it exploded. It was just like a gunshot. We all jumped out of our seats. Then there was a mess to clean up. Thorvald cried but Miss Hutchinson gave him some of her cocoa. Later she caught all the little ones banging down the lids of their pails, hoping they would explode too.

November 23

Travel on the Pink Bits

I've got my diary at school. This isn't exactly allowed. But Miss Hutchinson is busy with the little ones and the times tables so I don't think she will notice. We are supposed to be doing a grammar drill but I'm planning a round-the-world trip by looking at the big map. All the countries of the British Empire are pink so I'm hopping from one pink country to another. Here I go:

Canada, Newfoundland, United Kingdom (stop off to see Chivers and Auntie Lou and Uncle Alf and Auntie Millie and Baby Jack), Gibraltar, Malta, Cyprus, Anglo-Egyptian Sudan, Seychelles, India, Ceylon, Malaya, Borneo, Australia, Papua, Naura, Ellice Islands.

Later, at home

I was having such a good time on my journey that I didn't notice Nyla Snoop-Face Tattle-Tale Muir. She stopped by my desk on her way to the water pail and said, "Could you help me with the grammar drill? Oh, what a pretty notebook," in a voice loud enough for Miss Hutchinson to hear. So of course I got found out on the Ellice Islands and never got to Tristan da Cunha or back to Milorie.

Nyla is a pain in the you know where.

November 24

Talents

Today Miss Hutchinson said that everybody is good at something. I looked around and wondered if this were true. Hans is good at driving a car. Abel is good at making people laugh. Elizabeth is good at drawing. Gladys is good at reading. Nyla is good at being poisonous. George McLaren can stand up on the back of his horse. But then I looked at Vera Battrum. She isn't good at school, spelling, skipping, singing, running or sewing. I don't think Miss Hutchinson is right. This could be a question for Mr. Ambrose.

November 25

A Second Opinion

Mr. Ambrose says this isn't really an encyclopedia question but in his opinion Miss Hutchinson is right. But he doesn't know Vera.

I know that Mother thinks that I'm not good

at anything. But I am. I'm good at all of these:

1. Thinking of questions. (Mr. Ambrose says so.)
2. Having good bones. (Lorayne says so.)
3. Making up stories to scare myself. (I say so.)

November 26

Defeat

I'm wrong. Vera is good at something. Today she brought some nuts to school. She can crack them with her bare teeth.

December 4

Fairy Guest or How to Get Out of Serving Breakfast

A new guest in the hotel. He is a farm equipment salesman. He has hair growing out of his ears. I told Gladys that that meant he has fairy blood. Now Gladys is mad keen to serve his breakfast because she wants to be there in case he does something magic.

December 6

No Cowboy Christmas

This afternoon we didn't have arithmetic drill. Instead Miss Hutchinson said it was time to begin planning the Christmas concert. Ralph asked if they could do Cowboy Christmas again. Miss

Hutchinson asked what was Cowboy Christmas. Then everybody talked about last year when they did a skit where cowboys sit around a campfire singing Christmas carols. They had a real fire lit on the ashpan but Ralph's crepe paper chaps caught fire and Nels had to throw the pot of coffee over him to put it out. Ralph said it was keen and then he started singing, "Yippee-i-o, Ho ho ho," and everybody joined in. Then Miss Hutchinson had to bang her pointer on her desk. "No cowboys this year," she said.

Then she told us that this year we're going to do an acrostic act. She's going to write the letters of Santa Claus on big pieces of paper. (Santa Claus is Canadian for Father Christmas.) The little ones will hold them up, one letter at a time, and each letter will have a poem about it. Like, "S is for snow, da dum, da dum, da dum." And we have to make up the poems. She assigned the letters. I got one of the A's. Nyla Muir and Klaus Berg got the other A's. I thought right away of angel. No sooner had I thought of it than Nyla put up her hand and said could she do angel because she loves angels. Phooey. The two S's decided right away to do snow and Saskatchewan. I didn't have any other ideas for A so I went to the dictionary. The best word I found was apophthegm, which means a short saying, but it doesn't have that much to do with Christmas. Besides, what would rhyme with it?

Then Abel shot up his hand and said he had already finished his poem. He had C. Miss Hutchinson read it out:

C is for chilblains
We get them on our feet.
If you sit on the stove
You get them on your seat.

Of course Abel meant to be cheeky but he was sure surprised when Miss Hutchinson said that would be just fine.

We have until Friday to work on our poems. We're also supposed to think of songs or skits we would like to perform. I hope my poem turns out attractive and not asinine and that Miss Hutchinson adores it and does not abhor it.

December 7

Ivy the Hearing

Florence brought a little book to school with plays in it. At recess she asked me if I would like to be in one with her. There are five parts. The best thing is that she didn't ask Nyla. She asked Elizabeth, Vera and Nellie. Or maybe it is just because Miss Hutchinson told us today that Nyla is going to be mistress of ceremonies at the concert and maybe she wouldn't have time to also be in a play. But I think Florence likes me better than Nyla. It is probably wrong to feel so happy about this. Saints wouldn't. But I do.

We read the play out loud at lunchtime. It is very funny, about the five senses and Christmas. I get to be Hearing. I'll write down my piece here. Maybe it will help me remember it. Maybe the words will travel up my fingers to my brain.

When Christmas drew near
I wanted to hear
Everything everyone said.
But Grandma talked low
And Mum whispered so
It gave me a pain in the head.

We decided to make giant ears, nose, mouth, hands and glasses. I can imagine giant ears but I can't think how to make them. I wish there were some kind of magic stuff that you could mould into any shape. Like mud but clean and dries hard. And free.

No idea for A. At home it could be for the ass that Mary and Joseph ride on, but I'm not going to make that mistake again.

December 8

Fast Ears

I asked Mother about ears last night and this morning they were already made, sitting beside my bed when I woke up. She must have made them after I went to bed. They are perfect, huge, made of white cloth and stuffed with kapok so that they stick right up. They fasten to my head with a piece of elastic. If I move my head just a little bit they wiggle in a very comic way. I wore them to breakfast and Gladys laughed so much she inhaled her porridge. Dad told Mother they were a feat of engineering but Mother just harrumphed and said she hoped I would take them off before I served breakfast to the boarders. I don't know why Mother doesn't like it if you notice that she is being kind. If I'm kind I like people to notice right away and thank me.

Still no idea for A. I tried the dictionary again. I think I'll annihilate Nyla. Maybe I'll ask Mr. Ambrose.

December 9

Why Prepositions Can be Useful

Got it.

I did ask Mr. Ambrose and he said I should not limit myself to nouns.

A's for above
Where the bright star is glowing.
Christmas is coming,
The cattle are lowing.

I stole the last line from "Away in a Manger." I hope that's allowed. What's lowing, anyway?

December 10

Miss Hutchinson likes the "echo" of "Away in a Manger" in my poem. So it wasn't stealing but echoing.

December 11

Lowing is just mooing. There isn't much else to discuss about lowing so instead Mr. Ambrose told me about Percival Lowell, an authority on Mars.

Christmas card and letter from Ethel today. The noisy family moved out of number 107. Now there is a family with a boy that Ethel is sweet on. That was all she wrote about. She didn't mention Dot or anything else I told her about. Chivers did send love and purrs.

December 13

Christmas Concert Crisis

Nyla's mother came to school today. She is complaining because Miss Hutchinson told us not to wear our long underwear to the Christmas concert because it would not look good poking out from underneath our crepe-paper skirts. But Nyla's mother thinks it is dangerous for Nyla to take off her long underwear in winter, even for one evening. (Elizabeth and Florence and I wondered why Nyla even asked her mother. We certainly didn't. If you go around asking your parents for permission then you deserve what you get.)

Maybe Nyla won't be able to be in the concert and I can do angels after all.

December 14

Rats

The underwear crisis is solved. Miss Hutchinson is going to add one more layer of crepe paper to the bottom of the skirts and then Nyla can just roll up her long underwear. Still, she is going to look dumpy.

Lumpy dumpy Nyla Muir
She's a pill and that's for suir,
She's a disease
And there's no cuir.
Lumpy dumpy Nyla Muir.

Trying to think of my A poem seems to have made me think of rhymes all the time.

When Auntie Lou gave me this diary to record the most important things in my life she probably didn't know how good it would be for insults.

December 15

Letter from the Relatives

Today there was a letter from Auntie Millie. Mother read it out loud. Auntie Millie is expecting another baby! Baby Jack and Auntie Millie are living with Auntie Millie's parents in London but the pram-making business didn't work out so Uncle Alf has gone to the south coast for another job. Mother and Dad gave each other THE LOOK when Mother read out that bit. Baby Jack is walking and Auntie Millie looks forward to going up to Oxford Street at Christmas to see all the decorations.

Later I asked William about THE LOOK. He says he reckons that Uncle Alf has done a bunk and left Auntie Millie. I don't think that could be true. He would never leave Baby Jack and the baby on the way.

December 17

Dress Rehearsal

Today we didn't do any work in school. We just got ready for the concert. We had a fine time. The big boys stood on the desks and hung crepe-paper streamers from the roof. Mrs. Battrum came with white sheets to make curtains across the stage. A very talented artist used the Christmas stencils to make holly leaves and bells across the top of the blackboard. (Talented artist = me. Miss Hutchinson let me use the coloured chalks. I wish we could use them every day for our work. I think colours would really help with arithmetic drills.)

Then we pushed all the desks to the side and did a last rehearsal. I forgot my A poem after the first line. There were lots of other mistakes too. Miss Hutchinson said, "Bad dress rehearsal, good performance." But I don't know. When I think about standing up in front of everybody my insides hollow out. Toffee-Nose wore her mistress of ceremonies dress. It is made of layers and layers of crepe paper, like a rainbow. She said isn't it a shame that we all can't wear pretty dresses instead of just funny ears. I bit my tongue.

Then Mr. McLaren brought in the tree. We decorated it with paper chains and cut-out snowflakes and Miss Hutchinson made popcorn and we made that into strings. (And we ate some too.) Then we put the candles in the holders. Miss Hutchinson sent us home early.

December 19

Ears and Above

Nine o'clock in the morning and I'm still in my nightie. I'm writing this in bed. No church. We slept in because we were so late last night. Mother gave the boarders scones for breakfast so she didn't need me to help.

The concert was heaps of fun. The school didn't even look like the school with the candles and lanterns and the tree and the ceiling covered in dancing streamers. Before we started Miss Hutchinson gathered us together and told us to speak up, to have fun and not to set ourselves on fire. I remembered my ear piece and my A piece even though I felt my mouth was just saying the words and I was somewhere else. When Abel said his chilblain poem people cheered and stomped on the floor. They stomped again after "The Christmas Senses." And Dad went "Whoop!" which was a little embarrassing, but not too much. The little ones did their choral recitation of "The Christmas Cat" and it ended with Herman saying, "He purred in the manger and kept Jesus warm." Then all the mothers started crying. I almost did too.

Then there was the sound of bells outside and Santa Claus came in. He had presents for everyone. I got an orange and a bag of candy and a beautiful blue silk handkerchief. When Santa Claus called Gladys's name she was afraid to go and collect her present. She just held onto my leg. But then I told her it was just Father Christmas and she was fine. It turns out she didn't know that Santa Claus is just the Canadian name for Father Christmas. (Of course it was really Bill Bowler the butcher but I didn't tell her that.)

Then there was carol singing. Some of the little ones went to sleep on the desks. Then there was a big lunch with sandwiches and cakes and pie. It was after midnight when we got home.

Oh, I forgot. The biggest surprise. In between the Santa Acrostic and Ralph's homesteader recitation Miss Hutchinson got up and sang a song. She didn't tell us she was going to do it. It was called "The Ash Grove." Everyone was dead quiet when she sang. She looked like an angel from above.

December 20

Christmas Comes from Home

The Christmas parcel from Auntie Lou has arrived! Dad picked it up at the post office this morning. Mother made us wait until William came home from the store before we were allowed to open it at all. I nearly burst with waiting. What if I really had and bits of me had whizzed all around the room like the exploding cocoa from Thorvald's pail? It's like that funny poem that Dad recites about all the children who do naughty things and meet terrible ends. Here's mine, "Ivy Weatherall, The Girl Who Burst With Waiting":

dum di dum di dum di dum . . .
But though her family wailed and wept
The moral is that if you're kept
Waiting too long you might end up dead
Like The Girl Who Burst With Waiting.

There's something not right with line four. *You might meet the fate . . . You might end up in bits*

. . . That's better but still too long. Why are beginnings and ending of poems easier than middles?

But I didn't burst and when William FINALLY came home we opened up the box and it was a treasure chest. A fruitcake in a pretty tin with fancy paper round the edge and covered in marzipan with a piece of holly. A box with six glass Christmas balls. You can look inside them to a little scene. A tin of Lyle's Golden Syrup. (William said it made him think of collecting horse manure because he used to collect it on Halley Road with a Lyle's box. Of course it wouldn't be our family if somebody didn't bring that up.) A box of almonds. A box of Chivers Jellies. A bag of ribbon sweets and humbugs. A wrapped present for each of us. (Mine has edges like a book). Some English newspapers. A big pile of *Magnet*s.

Of course we have to save it for Christmas but Mother must have understood a little bit about bursting because she made a pot of tea and we all had a sliver of fruitcake. I eat cake then marzipan. William eats marzipan then cake.

Then William started flipping through the *Magnet*s. He used to buy one every Saturday at home. The *Magnet* is supposed to be a magazine just for boys, but I always liked it too. William started to read out loud a Famous Five story, with lovely Harry Wharton, and cheery Bob Cherry, studious Frank Nugent, Billy Bunter the fat boy, and all the other boys and masters at Greyfriars School. It was like meeting old friends from home. It was all there, the cricket game, the scrumptious tea, the jokes about Latin, Loder of the Sixth (that cad!), and the visit of a mysterious stranger. We wouldn't let William stop. Even Mother.

Then Harry asked, "Would Billy Bunter ever come to Milorie?" Harry was too young for the *Magnet* at home and he sometimes gets mixed up about stories and real things. But this made Dad and William start talking like the *Magnet*, but putting in everything about our life in Canada. Mother and I did it too:

"The chickens laid three dozen eggs today," said the venerable but distinguished John Weatherall. "Isn't that simply ripping!"

"Oh, my hat," said plucky Weatherall minor, "we have another elevator cleaning job tonight!"

"Oh, dash it all," said the glamorous Madame Weatherall, "the cutworms have destroyed the garden!"

"Oh, hard cheese!" said the beautiful but mysterious Miss Weatherall.

"Crikey!" said plucky Weatherall minor. "We seem to be snowed in by the blizzard. What shall we do?"

"Let's burn the house down!" said the equally plucky but mysterious Miss Weatherall.

"Dash it all!" said the glamorous and also mysterious Madame Weatherall. "I think that my brother Alf Jones has turned out to be a bit of a bounder!"

"Is there any more fruitcake?" Weatherall minor, the fat boy, enquired hopefully.

We started laughing so hard we started crying and the twins looked at us as though we were completely round the twist.

Later I thought of something. The twins won't really remember England at all when they grow up. It will just be stories to them. William and I will carry little bits of England around in us forever but the little ones won't. This made me feel quiet.

December 21

Planning Presents

Today is my day to make presents. For Mother and Dad I'm going to make a picture of the *Ausonia* at sea. For Harry a walnut-shell turtle. For Gladys a set of paper dolls. For William a pen-wiper.

Mother is doing secret knitting.

December 22

Present Plans Revised

I'm better with paper and glue than with sewing. The pen-wiper was horrid. I threw it away. Instead

I'm going to make William a three-cornered bookmark, using an envelope. I think I'll draw an octopus on it to remind him about deep-sea diving.

December 23

Cheering Up Gladys

Found Gladys crying today. She was worried that Father Christmas (the real one, not the one at the concert, she said) would not know that we have come to Canada. She cheered up when I told her that Father Christmas lives in Canada because that's where the North Pole is. So he obviously knows all about Canada and especially about the Weatheralls in Milorie. (Is that true? Is the North Pole in Canada? I can't ask Mr. Ambrose because he has gone away to his married son's for a few weeks.)

The Gilmours have invited us for Christmas dinner on Christmas Eve.

December 25

Deep and Crisp and Even

It is now Christmas afternoon. I feel happy and also a kind of sad that is almost like happy.

Christmas dinner was lovely, with roast duck and a Christmas pudding that Mr. Gilmour lit on fire. We had crackers with mottoes and silly paper hats. My motto was "The longest way round may be the shortest way home." After dinner we played charades. Mrs. Gilmour is very clever with charades. She was on our team and she made up a wonderful act for the word "pilgrim." First she was "pill." That was fairly easy. Then she was "grim," which made everyone laugh a lot because she kept pulling these dreadful faces. Then we all dressed up as pilgrims with bathrobes and wooden poles as our staffs and went walking around the room.

This morning we opened our presents and stockings. My present from Auntie Lou was a book. It is called *At the Back of the North Wind*. I don't want to start it too soon. I'm torturing myself by opening it and reading just one sentence on a page. Auntie Lou sent a book for William too. It is *The Adventures of Sherlock Holmes*.

My other presents were mitts and a box of watercolours. William got mitts and snowshoes. Gladys got mitts and a doll. Harry got mitts and a set of Tinkertoys. Now I know what Mother was mysteriously knitting!

Then we went to church. Even Dad came, and he hardly ever goes to church. It was carols and the Christmas story. I never thought before how the Christmas story is about travelling to a new place. Also, the holy land isn't very much like Milorie but I did wonder if the stable with the manger was a bit like a sod hut.

Goose and crackers and the shepherds and

oranges in our stockings. So many things are just the same about Christmas in Canada. It is making me sad for the things that are different, like no Auntie Lou and no Grandad.

William has gone off to try out his snowshoes. He has left a trail of dinted snow, just like in "Good King Wenceslas."

Paint or read? Christmas cake or humbugs?

Decisions, decisions.

January 3, 1927

Back to School

1927. Not quite as good to write as 1926. I like writing 9's and 6's best. I will like it when it is 1996. But by then I will be ancient (I can't be bothered to do the sum right now) and probably not keeping a diary.

Back to school. Nyla wore all new clothes, including a coat. She told us that she got a French ivory dresser set for Christmas that has a comb, brush, scissors, nail buffer, button hook and barrette. She also got three books. They are called *Just Patty, Patty Goes to College* and *Bab: A Sub-Deb.* She asked me what I got and I told her and she said, "Oh, practical presents." She said this in her pretending-to-be-nice voice.

I don't care though. The new year's good news is that I have a job! Today after school Miss

Hutchinson asked me if I would like the job of student janitor. This means coming to school early and lighting the stove. Ralph was doing it last term but he wasn't very responsible. It pays two dollars a month! I'm going to be extremely responsible.

January 4

My job

First day of my job. It was awfully cold and dark to get up so early but I said to myself, "To be up and doing is the maxim of a Canadian."

I got to school one hour early. Here's what I do: I clean the firebox by shaking all the ashes into the ashpan, which is under. Maybe I have to poke a bit with the poker. Then I put crumpled paper on the grate. Then I make a teepee of kindling wood. Then I get a match from the tin box in Miss Hutchinson's desk and light it. When it gets going I put in some coal. That part is fun. The next part isn't. I take the ashpan out. No matter how careful you are, the ashes fly into the air and make you cough. Then I take the ashes out to the ash heap behind the school. Then I sweep up around the stove. Then I collect up the ink bottles and put them on the stove to thaw.

By the time everyone came to school it was cozy. Miss Hutchinson commented on it. I feel like Catharine.

January 7

Shivers

Holy Moses! It suddenly got a lot colder. Went out this morning and it was like the cold wind went right into my brain. I wrapped my scarf around my face but breathing through it makes it wet and then it freezes and then there is a lump of ice-wool against your mouth. Also, my eyes watered and then the eyelashes froze together.

But still I got to school plenty early to light the stove and put the ink bottles on it to thaw. But it was so cold that the ink was still frozen at 9:30 so we had double the time of oral arithmetic drills and then we played The Grand Old Duke of York up and down the aisles to get warm. Even then Miss Hutchinson let us sit on our desks because the floor was so cold for our feet. But at least it was Friday so we had a story in the afternoon. Miss Hutchinson has started a new book. It is called *Sowing Seeds in Danny*. I like it because the main girl, Pearlie Watson, is twelve, and because the family lives in a boxcar and because they have twins, just like us. Also it is funny.

Dad got some work at the blacksmith's shop. I went over after school and he was sharpening a ploughshare. I like it there because it is so warm. He let me turn the blower on the forge. The metal turned white with heat and then I had to stand clear whilst Dad put it on the anvil and hammered away. Sparks were flying everywhere. Sweat was running down Dad's face. Then he lowered the tip of the ploughshare into the barrel of water and there was a huge hiss and steam.

Why is white hotter than red when frost and snow are white and fire and the sun are red? I could ask Dad but I think I'll save this question for Mr. Ambrose when he gets back because questions make him so happy.

We've got a new guest. It is the Rawleigh man. He goes around the country selling house things like medicine and spices made by the W.T. Rawleigh Company. He sniffs. I guess he doesn't have any medicine for sniffing. It was steak-and-kidney pie for dinner and he picked out all the kidney.

Tonight at supper everyone was talking about the cold. William said we should be grateful because at least there is absolutely no danger of malaria.

January 9

Bits and Pieces

Still very cold. Went to church this morning. Mr. Quigley read the story about when Jesus was twelve years old he wandered off and his parents found him in the temple, talking to the priests. I thought of the twelve-year-old boys I know, but I don't think Jesus was messy and loud like them. Maybe it isn't even proper to wonder about that.

At the Back of the North Wind is about a very poor boy named Diamond. His father named him after a horse. This is a good idea. I would be happy to name a daughter Dot.

Harry has made the Eiffel Tower with his Tinkertoys. He put the walnut turtle on the top.

January 12

Accident

There wasn't any school this afternoon. Abel cut his ear open on the swings at recess. Miss Hutchinson had to take care of him so we all got a half day off.

Abel was twirling, which is how it happened. Twirling is when you sit on the swing and twist around and around until the ropes are as tight as can be. Then you lie flat out and unwind. Twirling is forbidden but all the boys do it. But this time Abel was too close to the post and he bashed his ear on it. There was a lot of blood. Nyla screamed. Miss Hutchinson ran over and said for someone to get the first-aid kit. I did. Then she said for someone to go get Doc Johnstone and Florence did but Doc Johnstone was at a tonsils clinic in Stanton. So Miss Hutchinson tied on a bandage and then she took Abel to our house. Abel's mother is dead and his father would be working so there was no point taking him out to his farm. Also, Miss Hutchinson knows that Mother was a midwife in England so she's good with blood and accidents and that.

Miss Hutchinson and Mother looked at Abel's ear and said he would need stitches. Doc Johnstone was supposed to be back after dinner. We scrubbed the kitchen table and moved it over next to the window. Then we soaked a sheet in carbolic and laid it on the table. Abel was being awfully brave. He looked pale and woozy but he still kept making little jokes.

Then Mother said it was my job to mind the twins and I was so cross. My whole life I've wanted to see stitches and here they were going to happen in my own house and I was supposed to miss it. So I was very bold. I took the twins upstairs and played with them until I heard Doc Johnstone arrive. Then I bribed them with the last of my Christmas humbugs and the promise that I would play cats and dogs with them tomorrow for as long as they wanted if they would be good and quiet.

When I got downstairs Abel was lying on the table and Doc Johnstone was fitting a mask over his face. Mother saw me creep in and she gave me a look but she didn't say anything. Doc Johnstone instructed Mother to put a few drops of chloroform on the mask. Then Abel was to count backwards from twenty, but he only got to sixteen. Then his breathing got very slow. Doc Johnstone started stitching up his ear. It was very neat. He chatted. He said it was lucky that the ear cushioned the blow because Abel might have had a worse accident. Every so often he would tell Mother to put one more drop on the mask.

Then Abel stopped breathing. Mother and Doc Johnstone didn't seem to notice. But I heard it stop. I didn't know whether to speak up. But a voice just came out of me. Doc Johnstone whipped off the mask and started breathing into Abel's mouth and pushing on his chest. Abel started breathing again but he was restless and Mother had to hold him down whilst Doc Johnstone did the last stitches.

Afterwards he thanked me and said that his hearing wasn't what it used to be and that I was an alert girl.

When Abel woke up he started shivering, so Mother put him on the settee with lots of blankets, a hot water bottle and plenty of sweet tea. He will stay here tonight. Abel is always so jolly that I never thought before how sad it is that he doesn't have a mother. I don't think his father or brother would know about hot water bottles.

January 13

Mistake

Never make a rash promise to a six year old. Today I played cats and dogs with the twins for ages. Cats and dogs is the world's most tedious game. The twins made it up. One runs around mewing and the other runs around barking. After hours of this my brain turned into a bowl of junket.

January 15

Lucky Leftovers

Mr. Burgess gave William the bottom of a big tin of peanut butter. It was a bit dried up and he couldn't sell it. But if you mix it with syrup it is just fine. Mother and Dad don't like peanut butter. They think it is too strange. And they don't think it is proper food for the guests. Which is fine with me because I love it. On bread, toast and my finger. Almost as good as doughnuts and pumpkin pie.

January 17

Return of the Boarder

Mr. Ambrose is back from his son's. I was so happy when I came in from school and found him in the sitting room. I'll have to get into the way of thinking of questions again.

January 22

An Invitation

Today is Elizabeth's birthday. I'm invited out to the farm for dinner and to stay overnight. Hans will come and collect me with the sleigh. I bought Elizabeth a tin of Cashmere Bouquet face powder with my own money, from my job. I hope we get to listen to the radio.

January 23

Turning Twelve

We got to the Mullers' just in time for milking. It was already dark. I went out to the barn with Mrs. Muller and Elizabeth. I carried the lamp. The lamplight made long shadows across the snow in the yard. I can still remember how to milk. It was quiet in the barn. It felt like there was nothing else in the world. The kittens have grown up.

Then it was time for dinner. If I were the Duchess of Milorie or some other grand person I would eat Mrs. Muller's fried chicken every day of my life. Also chocolate cake.

After dinner we did listen to the radio. Then we went to bed and played corners. I think Elizabeth invented this game. You name each corner of the room with a boy's name. Then when you wake up in the morning the corner you are looking at is who you will marry. I used my four favourite names — Raymond, Edward, Stanley and Derek. When I woke up I was staring at Derek! Elizabeth was staring at Eugene. I don't know any Dereks. Elizabeth doesn't know any Eugenes. Somewhere they are growing up, waiting to meet us.

Now I'm home. Mother is grumpy. She wants me to peel potatoes. The Mullers have pictures on their walls. We don't. I wish I lived at the Mullers'.

Later

I take it back. I'm sitting in the kitchen and I can hear Dad getting the twins ready for bed. He's saying the poem he always used to say to me. He says it in a funny gloomy voice and lets you say the last word of each line.

Nothing to do but work
Nothing to eat but food
Nothing to wear but clothes
To keep you from going nude.

The twins have just yelled out "NUDE!" and now it sounds like Dad is chasing them around the room. I would rather have my Dad and no pictures or fried chicken than Elizabeth's stern father.

Wonder what Derek is like.

February 9

Indisposed

The reason that I haven't written in so long is that I have been sick. Last week on Tuesday I got really wet on my way home from school because of a snowball fight. The next morning I felt like I had thistles in my throat. Then I started coughing and coughing. Mother gave me hot lemon and honey to drink and put goose grease on my chest and a piece of camphor to wear around my neck, but nothing helped.

For days and days I just lay in bed and I didn't care about eating anything and I didn't even want to sit up to write. Sometimes I was very hot and once I thought the end of the bed was jumping up and down like laundry blowing in the wind. One night my ears hurt so much, like a hot knitting needle poking down my ear into my throat, that I couldn't stop crying. Dad lit his pipe and blew warm smoke into my ears. It helped some. Elizabeth brought me a new book but it hurt my eyes too much to read.

Today I feel better. Sort of floaty and I still can't go out to the outhouse, but I'm a bit hungry and I might start reading the book. Tired now.

February 10

Tiny Ivy

I would like to know what is going on when a person is sick. I would like to shrink and go in a tiny car down my throat and just have a look at what's making it so thistly and into the part that starts the coughing. Mother says the next time Doc Johnstone has a tonsils clinic I must go and have mine out.

February 11

Injustice

Last night I had a fight with Harry. He used my paints without asking and left the tops off three of the tubes and they dried up. I yelled at him and then I got in trouble because Mother said I was making noise and disturbing the guests. She didn't even want to hear my side of the story. Just because Harry is little he gets away with everything. He is spoiled.

Mother said if I was well enough to raise a ruckus I was well enough to go back to school. I was glad I went back today because we made valentines. Miss Hutchinson gave us some lovely red paper. Elizabeth taught me how to make paper lace. It is like making snowflakes. Miss Hutchinson put some poems on the blackboard for the little ones to copy. Abel was laughing to himself so I have an idea that he is making up his own. The big boys didn't want to do it but Miss Hutchinson was stern. Then we decorated a big box to put the valentines in. Everybody made one for everybody so the box is very full.

Miss Hutchinson did my janitor job for me whilst I was sick. She said she was glad I was back because she was "fed up to the eyeteeth with ashes." What are eyeteeth? Question for Mr. Ambrose.

February 14

Hearts

Valentine's Day. We had games and cookies at school and almost no lessons. Abel's card for me said:

Please be mine.
Think you're swell.
Else I'll push you.
Down the well.

There was one lovey-dovey one that said "From Derek." At first I was astonished. Then I realized Elizabeth had done it as a joke.

When I got home Mother told me a story about my valentines when I was three years old. I got valentines in the mail but the flu epidemic was on and all the mail had to be put in the oven to sterilize it, so any germs would be killed. And the oven was too hot and my valentines burnt up. Mother said I cried and cried. But I don't remember this.

February 16

Nostrils

This might be a short write. I'm minding the twins whilst Mother is at Homemaker's Club. They are playing cats and dogs.

I nearly got kept in at school today. Thank goodness I didn't. I got in trouble with Miss Hutchinson because I was showing Elizabeth about smelling through one nostril and then the other. If you sniff something through your right nostril it usually smells better than if you sniff it through your left nostril. I was using my pencil. Left nostril it smelled okay, but right nostril it smelled terribly nice, all cedar.

Elizabeth tried it and it worked for her too. But then Nellie asked what we were doing and then she tried it but her left nostril did a kind of whistle, which gave us all the giggles. Then Miss Hutchinson came over and asked were we doing our spelling drill and of course we weren't. Then Nellie said we were smelling through our nostrils. Then Miss Hutchinson asked who started it so I confessed. She said I had to stay in after school and write lines.

After school Miss Hutchinson asked me what I

thought I should write. I tried to make it as short as possible so I said, “I will not practise smelling through my nostrils in school.” She was sort of smiling and told me to go ahead.

But I only wrote it three times before she started to giggle. Then she messed my hair and said, “What they don’t teach you in normal school.” Then she told me to go home.

On the way out, though, she said that because it was after school we could try it one more time. Then she took a little bottle of perfume out of her handbag and dabbed some on my wrist. Then she tried sniffing. But it didn’t work for her. Now I smell like Miss Hutchinson. I like it.

Oh-oh. I don’t hear any cats or dogs. It is usually bad news when the twins are quiet.

February 17

The Twins Get Another Idea

It was bad news. They had taken all the coal out of the coal pail and spread it all around the kitchen and Harry was sitting with the coal scuttle over his head.

I think when they play cats and dogs they stop being human and turn into animals.

February 24

The Unmentionable

William and Dad have a new job. It isn't very nice. At night they go and shovel out outhouses. They move the outhouse then they shovel out the . . . I've stopped for a minute because I can't write that word down. Even though this diary is absolutely and totally and completely private it would still be vulgar. Mother says that the use of vulgar words is the mark of an impoverished mind. What I don't understand is that everybody knows the words and doesn't everybody use them inside their heads? Is it possible to be vulgar on the inside and not vulgar on the outside? Maybe not everybody uses them inside their heads. Probably Nyla Muir doesn't. But it is hard not to think of this word, especially as it goes so well with "shovel."

That was a digression.

Then they shovel out the contents of the hole and put it on a sledge and take it out of town to the dumping ground. (They call the sledge a stone boat here. Another funny Canadian word.) Dad is funny about it. He calls the outhouses the Houses of Parliament and the sledge his coach and four. He also says, "The work is dirty but the money is clean." But William is quiet and a bit miserable looking. I think he must hate it because he is the cleanest boy I know. Fingernails and that.

I just looked at my own fingernails. They are not models of good grooming.

February 26

Check and Mate

Mr. Ambrose is teaching William to play chess. He tried to teach me but I can't be bothered. Here's what you have to think like when you play chess:

"If I do this then he might do that and then I could do this. But what if he doesn't do that?" By the second "he might, so I could" I find myself thinking about lunch, or why my big toe is so itchy.

But William seems to love it. He gets this dreamy look on his face and he isn't blinking so much.

March 1

No Skates

March. Three days until my birthday. In this family our birthdays are all bunched up in the spring. (Except March isn't spring in Saskatchewan, it is still blinking cold.) I'm first. Then the twins on April 2nd. Then William at the end of April. I like having my birthday in a month that is a word.

Mother and Dad say there is no money for birthday presents this year. There isn't any work for Dad at the blacksmith's. And we only have Mr. Ambrose staying in the hotel. Dad says it will be better soon because there will be work for him, and William will have finished paying off Uncle Alf's debts. Mother says there is a chance that the Chautauqua talent will board with us when they come in June. Mother says that would really put us on our feet. But until we're on our feet, no birthday presents. I was hoping for skates.

I wonder why we're not like the man who came to Canada with 27 cents and ended up with 200 cows. Or even like the family with the fat baby with a carrot as big as his head. Dad has all those things they said in the book: health, industry and good habits. So do William and Mother. Uncle Alf didn't make a go of it, but I guess he didn't have good habits or industry. Maybe it is just that we haven't been here a year yet. Dad says our ship is bound to come in any day now. When he says that Mother flicks him on the skull and says, "And where is a ship supposed to dock in Saskatchewan?"

But then she says to count our blessings because at least we're not hungry and we have a roof over our heads. When she says that I think of walking around with this little roof over my head, like an umbrella.

When I imagine skates I think I wouldn't mind being a bit hungry.

March 2

A Good Idea

Dad says that he has been giving birthdays another thought and we can have anything we want as long as it doesn't cost money. Harry said did he mean anything? Dad said anything that wouldn't land us in jail or in the hospital.

A brilliant idea has come to me:

It doesn't cost anything.

It is not against the law.

It is not dangerous.

I'm going to tell William and the twins. I hope the twins can keep a secret.

I tried folding my hair up but it didn't look short. It just looked folded.

March 3

Enter the Flapper

I am a new person. I am twelve years old and . . .

I HAVE A BOB!

I love it. The air blows around my neck and ears. I can do anything I want, even stand on my head, and no hair gets in my eyes. My head feels lighter than a hot-air balloon. The sun shone in my ears and I felt like it was shining into my brain.

I gave all my hair ribbons to Gladys. She wore

three at the same time and said she felt like it was her birthday.

Mrs. Muller did it. I went over yesterday and I told her about the birthday treat and the rules and she agreed to do it. She put me on a chair in the kitchen and snipped away. The sound of scissors cutting into hair is a delicious sound. When I saw my hair falling to the floor I did get a bit scared. What if it was a mistake? But it wasn't. When I look in the mirror I almost don't know myself.

When I got home I walked into the kitchen. Mother was washing up and William and the twins were there. The twins got big eyes and Harry nearly said something but Gladys put her hand over his mouth. When Mother turned around she screamed. (Not a really loud scream — more like "Eeeeek.") And I said, right quick, that it was my birthday treat. And William said, "It didn't cost anything." And Gladys said, "It's not a crime." And Harry said, "It's not bad for you." Then Mother started to laugh and she had to dry her eyes on her apron. Then she came over and spun me around a few times and then she knocked all our heads together and said we were cheeky monkeys.

When Dad came home he said that I looked so grown up that he felt like an old man. Then he walked around all stooped over and talking in a quavery voice about his flapper daughter.

I can't wait for tomorrow to show everyone at school.

Mother made a scrumptious chocolate cake. It had candles. I made a wish. Does it spoil your wish if you tell it to your diary? Probably.

March 4

Everybody likes my hair. Except Nyla who is pretending she hasn't noticed.

March 7

Coming Event

Elizabeth told me that there is going to be a box social at the school on Saturday. Here's what it is: All the ladies and girls make a lunch for two and they put them in boxes. They decorate the boxes. Then all the men come to an auction where the box lunches are auctioned off. Whatever lunch box you buy, you get to have lunch with that lady. But nobody is supposed to know who made which box. The money is to buy a piano for the school. I asked Mother if I could make a box lunch and she said it sounded daft but yes I could. I looked in the *United Farm Women Cookbook* for ideas and I am going to make jumbles biscuits and black-eyed Susan sandwiches. For the sandwiches you cut a piece of brown bread in a circle. Then you spread it with grated cheese with a little butter mixed in. Then you cut a smaller piece of white bread into a doughnut shape and put it on top. Then you fill the hole with raisins. You stick them into the cheese. I think they will look swell.

March 11

Elizabeth came over this afternoon after school and we made our boxes for the box social. Elizabeth made paper flowers for hers. I had some dark blue paper from a roll of cotton batting so I got the idea to decorate mine like the sky, with yellow suns and moons and stars on blue. They look very fine.

March 12

Mortified

I am mortified. It is all the fault of that dratted box social.

It started out well. I made my jumbles and my black-eyed Susan sandwiches and they turned out fine.

But I rue the day, the hour and the minute I got the idea to decorate my box like the sky.

My box was the third to be auctioned. The first fetched ten cents. It was made by Mrs. Shepherd and bought by Mr. Quigley. The second fetched seventeen cents. It was made by Nyla, and her Dad bought it. Then mine. All the single fellows started bidding and they went daft. They wouldn't stop. Everyone started whooping and stamping their feet. Elizabeth grabbed my hand and nearly squeezed it to death. I couldn't figure it out. Finally the auction man said, "Going once, going twice, SOLD, to Lars Thorson for ten dollars." Ten dollars! Then Mr. Thorson went up to get the lunch and the auction man said, "A lovely lunch made by young Ivy Weatherall." And Mr. Thorson stopped dead in his tracks, stunned. He looked like he had been hit by a baseball bat. And everybody laughed.

Later another box with stars came up for auction. And the auction man said how it was a coincidence, another starry box. And everyone laughed again. And then there was the bidding and we found out it was Miss Hutchinson's box.

And finally I understood. All the bachelors must have found out somehow that Miss Hutchinson's box was going to have stars on it and they are all sweet on her. So they thought my box was hers. I wanted to die or disappear. But I couldn't. I had to have lunch with Mr. Thorson.

He was very nice and asked me about school and said he liked the sandwiches. But it was MORTIFYING. He's a grown-up man. Some of the lads came by and ribbed him. There was a dance after but I said I didn't feel well and I came home. I think I'll stay here forever.

March 13

Yesterday is Gone

I am going to draw a veil over the box social. I thought about tearing out that page in the diary so I will never read about it by mistake again, but I don't want to spoil the book.

Disappeared, erased, gone, vanished. That's all the words I know for that.

Today in church it was the story of the Prodigal Son. Afterwards Elizabeth was sad because she said it sounded just like her family except with a different ending. If Gerhard came home, Mr. Muller wouldn't kill the fatted calf for him. Gerhard is playing with a band in Calgary now, in a big hotel. He writes, but Mr. Muller doesn't read the letters.

March 15

Springtime in Saskatchewan

Today Miss Hutchinson has announced a contest. She said that we should write a descriptive piece about spring. The prize is going to be a little carved windmill. Mr. Gilmour made it. It is very cunning and I would like to win it.

Not much sign of spring. It is still blinking cold

and the ground is frozen solid but Miss Hutchinson says we live in hope and console ourselves with literature. She said we had to use a lot of descriptive words. Today we got to work on our pieces. Here's mine:

The bright purple crocuses
are blooming merrily in the pasture.
The merry musical meadowlark
sings her lovely song to the azure welkin.
The curious winsome gopher wakes up
from his long winter's sleep
and pops up his little furry head.
Spring has come to Saskatchewan.

Welkin means sky. I found it in a poem in our reader. It is a very poetic word. I'll bet it gets me extra points.

Abel Butt showed me his piece. It is called "Gumbo." (Gumbo is Canadian for mud.) It talked about pigweed and ragweed and stinkweed and how the road has turned to greasy gumbo. He said that the crows cawing sounded like Mr. Willis who sits in front of the livery stable, coughing before he spits. He said that you know it is spring when Nyla Muir finally takes off her long underwear.

I don't think Abel will win because he doesn't have many descriptive words. (But it is true about Mr. Willis.)

March 16

Another Use for the Eaton's Catalogue

Today Elizabeth and I played a game she invented, called point. You open to a page in the catalogue and then you say 1, 2, 3 and then you both point to your favourite thing. Then I taught her pinbook. You hold a pin in one hand and you flip through the catalogue with the other and you stab something. Then you have to make up a story about the thing that you stabbed. One trick is to flip quickly through the farm implements sections because there aren't that many stories you can make up about a cream separator. But today Elizabeth got a really good one, a size 44 Stylish Stout Figure corset with what the catalogue called coiled comfort boning. She made up a story about a really fat lady called the Roly Poly Lady and she got me laughing so hard I snorted my milk up my nose.

Another good thing about Canada: Elizabeth.

Nyla is acting all know-it-all about the spring description contest. Miss Hutchinson announces the winner tomorrow.

March 17

Nyla Triumphs

Nyla won the contest. Rats. It pains me to say this but her piece was very clever. It was a poem and it was like a famous poem that is in our reader, "I must go down to the sea again," except it was, "I must go down to the farm again." She acted all surprised and humble. Nyla acting humble is a truly horrid sight.

March 18

Abel Sad

Something is wrong with Abel. Today at recess the boys were practising walking on their hands and Abel didn't even want to try. Maybe he is sad that he didn't win the poetry contest. But usually he is a very bounce-back kind of person.

March 20

Warning

If you are reading this diary then you are a lowlife. But if you read this part you are worse. You deserve to crawl on your belly like a worm. If you read this may your sorrows be long and your days short, may your stewpot never be full and your tankard always empty. This is the curse of the fairies that Grandad taught me. (As student janitor I have another Canadian bit to add: May your coal scuttle always be empty and your ashpan always full.)

The secret is that Nyla Muir copied her toffee-nosed prize-winning poem. Here's how I found out: On Friday Harry was in the hayloft of the school barn and he brought home some papers from there. They have old *Leaders* piled up there. Last night I was sitting reading one and THERE IT WAS. "I must go down to the farm again." It is by some fourteen-year-old in Grenfell, Saskatchewan. Word for word!

Nyla Muir is a liar and a sneak and a . . . what's that word for poem-copyer? Polygamist? (What good is a dictionary if you don't know the word to begin with?)

I have two questions:

1. What should I do?

2. What was Nyla doing in the hayloft of the school barn?

March 21

Brain Rack

I told Elizabeth. I had to. Keeping a secret like that to yourself is like holding your breath. You have to breathe out or you would die or burst. We can't tell Miss Hutchinson because that would be telling. But it is NOT FAIR if Nyla gets to keep that nice windmill and all the glory.

Today I stared at the back of her head, beaming the words "I know what you did" at her. But she didn't notice.

I am racking my brains thinking what to do.

P.S. This is NOT just because I want to win the prize myself, even though Elizabeth says I should have because of my many descriptive words. This is about justice.

March 25

Injustice

Life is not fair. Miss Hutchinson is not a nice teacher. Elizabeth is not my friend. I hate Canada and as soon as I'm fourteen I'm going to get a job and make enough money to go home to England.

Nyla Muir steals a poem. Nyla Muir cheats. Nyla Muir gets a prize she doesn't deserve. Nyla Muir commits plagiarism. (That's the word for stealing a poem. Miss H. used it.) But — who gets in trouble? Me!

I can't write any more. I'm so angry I just want to stick this pen right through the paper.

Later

I went out and kicked the fence. Now I can continue.

Last night, Elizabeth (my former friend) and I decided that the best thing to do would be to cut the poem out of the paper and put it in Miss Hutchinson's desk. Then she would know that

Nyla cheated but she wouldn't know who told her. So yesterday at recess whilst Miss H. was out playing with the little ones we sneaked into the school and put the poem in her desk.

When we got back from recess Miss H. didn't say anything, but just before lunch she asked Nyla to stay behind and help her with the blackboard erasers over lunch. Elizabeth and I didn't look at each other but WE KNEW. Nyla took a long time coming out with the erasers, but when she did she was really whacking them against the shed wall. Chalk dust was flying everywhere.

So I thought justice was done. But then, after lunch, Miss Hutchinson pulls the poem out of her desk and holds it up. Not so that you can see what's on it, just like a little flag. Then she says, "Somebody in this class knows about this piece of paper. I expect that person to come see me privately."

I just stared at my desk. Somebody named Howard once wrote his name on the desk in little ink dots. I tried to think of how many words you could make with the letters of Howard.

After school Elizabeth said that we should go and see Miss H. But I said why are we suddenly the bad ones? If we just left it for a few days then everybody would forget about it. Then we had a fight and I called Elizabeth a goody-goody and a teacher's pet and she called me a coward and said if I don't go on Monday she's going to go alone.

But she's not going to tell Miss H. that I'm part of it. So, of course I felt really bad and told her that she was a blackmailer.

I wish I'd never found the darn poem.

We had tripe for dinner. Mother made me eat it. I hate tripe. The twins called me a crosspatch.

March 28

A New Week

I take it back. Miss Hutchinson is a nice teacher. Elizabeth is back to being my friend. Nyla Muir is still a toffee-nosed creepy plagiarist though.

I had a horrid weekend. Friday night I couldn't sleep because I had tripe in my stomach. Saturday night I couldn't sleep because I kept thinking how lonely it is not having a best friend.

So this afternoon I went out to Elizabeth's and then we both came into town and went to the teacherage and told. Miss Hutchinson said it was brave of us to come and what she wanted to say was that putting the poem in her desk was not the best thing to do. We should have told Nyla quietly and given her a chance to own up. What we did was sneaky. But now it was over and we wouldn't refer to it again. Then she gave us a cup of tea in really pretty cups and showed us her picture postcard collection. Miss Hutchinson has little bits of ribbon in her picture frames. It looks very smart.

I know we're not supposed to talk about this again but I don't think talking to your diary really counts. There is a hole in Miss Hutchinson's line of thinking. What are the chances that Nyla would have confessed? I would say 0%. What are the chances that Nyla would just have hated us even more than she does now? I would say 100%. Final question and then my lips are sealed on the subject of Nyla's poem forever. Even if I was on the medieval torture instrument I would not say another word after this one:

What was Nyla doing in the school barn?

April 1

Fools

Whilst we were having breakfast today there was a sound like a pig outside the kitchen window. Mother said, "Cor, what is that?" Turned out it was Dad playing an April Fools' trick. He got punished by having to serve breakfast to the boarders and do the washing up.

At school Miss Hutchinson had a mouse in her desk but she wasn't one bit scared. Then just before recess there was an explosion in the stove. Somebody had put a .22 shell in there and it went off. Nobody owned up and Miss H. said she hoped we knew that April Fools ends at noon. Then she gave up and read us some stories about tricking.

There was a very funny one about a giant who dresses up like a baby.

April 2

Two Turn Seven

The twins decided for their birthday present they wanted to be treated like a king and queen all day. They wore their bathrobes and paper crowns and ordered us around. Everyone played along. Mr. Ambrose was especially good. He walked backwards out the door because he said that you must never turn your back on royalty. The twins ate all their meals in tiny pieces out of the celery dishes. (The celery dishes are yellow glass and they pretended they were gold).

Mother said that she wished that birthdays ended at noon like April Fools. At five o'clock Harry ordered us all to be executed and Mother said she would welcome the escape.

April 3

Selling Up

Abel is moving. His father told us after church today. He said the hail ruined his crop last fall and it was the last straw and he just can't make a go of it. They are going to move to Vancouver where maybe Mr. Butt can get a job in a sawmill. I hauled

Abel off to talk. He wasn't jokey at all. He said his dad told him that in Vancouver they have trees along the streets that bloom in the spring and that the blossoms fall like pink snow. But he said he still didn't want to leave.

I thought if you had a farm you were all set. We don't even have a farm. I wonder if we're going to make a go of it. But we do have Mother and the hotel (with THREE guests at the moment) and William and the store. Abel and his dad have only each other. I will miss him. He is jolly and a better poet than a certain plagiarist I could mention, but won't.

April 4

***?!#*&#! (That is a bad word)*

Mother has a broken wrist and it is all my fault.

The other day Mr. Ambrose was talking about magnets. I must be a magnet for trouble. Invisible bits of trouble float around and when they get near me they jump right onto me.

This morning Mother asked me to go down to the cellar to get some potatoes. Whilst I was down there William called me and said, "Come quick!" So I raced up the ladder and the kitchen door was open and William was outside. He said I should come with him quick, so I did, around to the back of the house.

There was a gopher. The first one of spring. Big teeth. Bright eyes. It was like seeing an old friend.

Then we heard a crash and a yell from inside. I knew right away what had happened. I had left the cellar trapdoor open. The only question was who.

It was Mother. She was carrying a tray in from the boarders' breakfast and she fell right down into the cellar.

We helped her up but the damage is:

1. two broken plates
2. one broken teacup
3. one broken wrist

I won't write down what she said about me. It is all true. I thought everything would be better when I was twelve years old. When does it get better?

April 7

Too busy to write. Helping with washing and baking and minding. Mother says I have to be her right hand.

April 12

Elementary, My Dear Watson

Snow day! I knew there was snow even before I opened my eyes. How did I know?

Like Mr. Sherlock Holmes I used my powers of observation and deduction.

1. I could see the brightness of the room through my eyelids.

2. I heard William talking in the kitchen. Usually he has left for the store by the time I wake up.

3. Gladys was standing at the window, jumping up and down and singing, "Snow, snow, snow."

It is not just snow but deep snow and blowing so we can't go to school. Good. It was going to be a grammar bee. Grammar has a lot of ways to be wrong and hardly any ways to be right. After I finish this I'm going to write to Auntie Lou and tell her that here it is five days before Easter and it is snowing. She will be amazed. I guess Elizabeth wasn't exaggerating when she said that you have to keep your long underwear on until the 24th of May. I'll bet that gopher has gone back underground.

April 13

Miracle

Four o'clock in the afternoon. I am so tired that my head wants to roll off my neck but I just want to say that the most amazing thing happened today. And yesterday.

April 14

The Arrival

It is five o'clock in the morning. Everybody in the house is asleep. Now I can tell the story.

On Tuesday, the snow day, I did write to Auntie Lou. Then I helped Mother make bread. I had to do the kneading. We made cloverleaf rolls for a treat. The snow got heavier and heavier and blowier and blowier (blowier is probably not grammar but Miss Hutchinson is not going to be reading this). I remembered the day last fall when I burnt up the chairs.

After the bread was set to rise I went upstairs to play juicy meat with the twins when it all started. (If you want to know how to play juicy meat see the P.S. Otherwise just go on with this story.) Mother came upstairs and she looked so serious that I thought we were going to get in trouble. (Juicy meat can be quite a noisy game.) But she just told the twins to go down to the kitchen and then she sat on the edge of the bed and told me she needed me. She told me that Mr. Nygaard was downstairs and that Mrs. Nygaard had started to have her baby and that the doctor was snowed in at a farm near Stanton and couldn't come. Mr. Nygaard needed Mother to come because he knew she had been a midwife in England. "But," said Mother, "I can't manage with my wrist. Mr. Nygaard thinks I need to come straight away and the snow is getting heavier by the minute. Mrs. Johnstone has gone to Stanton with the doctor and I don't have time to fetch Mrs. Gilmour. I need you to come and help. Do you think you can do it?"

How do you know if you can do something you've never done? I felt scared. I said, "I think so."

Then Mother got very brisk. She got out her carpetbag and I went around and collected things like scissors, soap, the ragbag and the oilcloth from our table. At the last minute Mother put the cloverleaf rolls in a bag. "Don't know what we'll find," she said. We put on our warmest clothes. I borrowed William's jacket and toque. The only good thing about the walk to the Nygaards' was that the wind was behind us, pushing us along.

We arrived at the Nygaards' farm. Mother went right into the bedroom. I unpacked the bag. When Mother came out she said it would be a while yet and that Mr. Nygaard should go out and water the stock. Then she made a cup of tea and we sat for a minute and she talked to me. She was serious but not cross. She said that it took a long time for a baby to be born, that there was going to be pain and mess, but that we must keep our minds on the fact that we had a job to do, to help Mrs. Nygaard as much as we could. Then she said it was a good thing that she had never been one for telling us that babies were found under gooseberry bushes or any of that nonsense and we both laughed a little bit.

It's true. I did know how babies are born. But I didn't really know. Not like you know when you've been there and seen it. It was very surprising and amazing and scary and happy and I don't know what other descriptive words to use.

We arrived at the farm about three o'clock in the afternoon and the baby was born at ten the next morning. An afternoon, evening, night and morning and everything got mixed up in time. First thing we did was cut our fingernails and scrub our hands until they were pink. Then we remade Mrs. Nygaard's bed with the oilcloth under the sheet. Nobody said this was because there was going to be blood and things but I figured it out and it made my stomach jump up and down a bit. Then Mother got me to sew clean rags around fat bundles of sheets of newspaper. It wasn't good sewing but nobody cared.

Sometimes Mrs. Nygaard lay on the bed, and sometimes she walked around and Mother said things about breathing and told her she was a "good girl." Mother was different. She didn't once tell Mrs. Nygaard to buck up.

I did ordinary things like making tea and buttering rolls and feeding the cat and sweeping the kitchen. When Mrs. Nygaard cried or moaned I felt scared. Mr. Nygaard came in and held her hand and said things in Norwegian. But when the baby really started to come everything got really busy and I stopped feeling scared. Mr. Nygaard started to look a bit peaky, though, and Mother sent him out to the kitchen to boil some string. When he left Mother smiled at me and said, "A fainter. You can tell. Best to send them off to boil something."

Then we saw the top of the baby's head (black hair!) and Mother told me what to do and I just did it. And the baby slithered out and Mother said "It's a girl" and told me how to clean the face and hold the baby up and the baby cried (loud!) and Mother wrapped her in a blanket and handed her to Mrs. Nygaard who cried too (soft) and Mr. Nygaard came in and then he cried.

Later I got to hold the baby in my lap and rub her with baby oil and then rub it off. I just kept thinking, "They are letting me do this." Whilst I was cleaning her she grabbed my finger. She had the most amazing tiny fingernails. I never thought of that before, how we are born with fingernails.

When it was all over and everything was cleaned up and the baby was cuddled up with a hot water bottle Mr. Nygaard said, "Listen." And then we heard the dripping. The snowstorm was over and already the snow was melting. I looked out the window into the bright sun and then I looked back at Mrs. Nygaard and the baby in bed and they looked like a Christmas card.

When we were walking home I was so tired that

I looked down at my feet and they didn't look as though they belonged to me. Like it was some sort of joke that they were attached to the ends of my legs. My brain was too tired to think much, but I did have room for one thought. I remembered that in the whole night Mother had never once said I was clumsy or dreamy. She hadn't clicked her tongue once. Then when we were nearly home she squeezed my shoulder and said thank you to me for my SPLENDID help and then she said it was obvious that I had a gift for nursing.

If my feet had belonged to me I would have done a jig all over the yard.

April 15

Ivy's Official Juicy Meat Guide

I read over yesterday and realized I had forgotten the P.S. In the game juicy meat you chase somebody all over the house threatening to bite them and saying "Juicy Meat." The twins invented it. They love it.

April 16

Modifiers

A miracle happens and the world just goes plodding on. The grammar bee was postponed, not cancelled. I got bumped out in the first round yesterday because I didn't remember that adverbs modify adjectives. The fact that I am a splendid person with a gift doesn't butter any parsnips with Miss Hutchinson when she's doing grammar.

April 18

Goodbye This Book

This book is nearly finished. William bought me a new one. Mr. Burgess gave him a raise at the store and he bought us all presents. William is the best brother in the galaxy. But I'm going to write small so I can fit in this one last thing because it should go in the same book as everything else about coming to Canada. Today Mother and I went to visit the Nygaards. The baby is lovely. Mrs. Nygaard told me that they've chosen a name for her. They are going to call her Ivy. After me. She is going to be my namesake. Mr. Nygaard said that she is a little Canadian Ivy. Then Mother said that I am a big Canadian Ivy.

Later

I just read over the first part of this diary. On May 19th, 1926, I said that the only thing the same about my new address was me and The World.

Now I am:

Ivy Doris Weatherall
The Bank Building
Milorie, Saskatchewan
Canada
North America
The World

Except now I'm not the same Ivy Weatherall. So the only thing the same is living in The World.

Epilogue

Ivy did not become a deep-sea diver. But, just as her mother said, she did turn out to have a gift for nursing. Pursuing her education was tough for Ivy. In 1929 Canada entered the Great Depression. Times were tough everywhere, but they were worst on the prairies. The economic depression coincided with years of terrible weather for farmers. But Ivy persevered and managed to get her high school education, and then to move to Vancouver to go to nursing school. She loved life as a student. She made many friends among her fellow students. She hiked the local mountains.

Most of all, she discovered a passion for science. When she graduated as a registered nurse she got the highest marks in all of Canada. After nursing for several years she was given a scholarship to return to university for a nursing degree. She eventually became a professor of nursing at McGill University in Montreal. Her many nieces and nephews adored visiting her. The fact that she owned a succession of sports cars might have had something to do with her popularity as an aunt.

William spent several years working as a clerk in various stores, in Milorie and later in Calgary. During the Depression, when work was scarce, his was often the only family income. In his mid-twenties he joined the Royal Canadian Mounted Police and was posted to the far north. He spent his whole career in the land of the midnight sun and was very happy there. He married and had four children. His son Gordon lived with his Aunt Ivy when he went to university in Montreal.

When World War II began, Gladys followed in her father's seagoing footsteps and joined the Royal Canadian Navy. Here she met the man who was to become her husband. Later they settled in southern Ontario, where they started a nursery business.

In this far-flung family, Harry was the only one who stayed in Saskatchewan, settling in Regina, where he worked in radio, then got in on the ground floor of the exciting new invention of television.

Abel and his father did make it to Vancouver, where Mr. Butt remarried — a widow with several small children. Abel did very well in the role of adored older brother. He and Ivy kept in touch for their whole lives.

No Weatheralls remained in Milorie. The town itself, the setting for the beginning of Ivy's great adventure, disappeared in the early 1960s. You will not find it on a current map of Saskatchewan. But in the memories of Ivy, William and the twins, and in the stories they tell their families, it is still there — a grain elevator pointing to the sky, summer dust between the toes, the taste of saskatoon berry pie, and the view clear through to half past tomorrow.

Historical Note

In 1926, 104,741 people left their homes to come to Canada. They were a variety of nationalities — French, Irish, Scandinavian, German, Scottish, Czech and others — but the largest immigrant group in that year were the English. Like immigrants everywhere, and at all times, they came in hope. In the new land they hoped for prosperity, freedom and adventure. English immigrants were also leaving behind what was, for many of them, an impossible situation at home. Working-class men went off to fight in the first World War with the government's promise that when they returned there would be good jobs. For many, that promise turned out to be hollow and they returned home to poverty, unemployment and limited prospects for the future. Bitter and frustrated, some decided to try their fortunes across the seas, in the new world.

But why did they choose Canada?

Many families chose to come to Canada because they had connections among relatives and friends who had already immigrated. Before World War I many English people came to the Canadian west as homesteaders. They were given 160 acres of land for just ten dollars, with the agreement that they would build a house and cultivate the prairie. These adventurous, hard-working people raised families and created communities. English people who were considering a new home in later years knew that there would be people in Canada with whom they shared language and history.

In the 1920s the Canadian and British governments actively sought British settlers, but not with much success. Ottawa consequently had to turn to continental Europe for potential immigrants. Although these people helped build western Canada, many established settlers of Anglo-Canadian background feared that the new immigrants might make Canada what they disparagingly called a "mongrel" nation.

The railway also played a part in this wave of immigration. The Canadian Pacific Railway had land to sell and they needed buyers. To recruit immigrants, governments organized and funded incentive programs such as the Empire Settlement Act of 1922 and the 3,000 Families Scheme. There was a program to bring over British school teachers to the Canadian west, plus the Canadian Cottages Agreement of 1924, in which the British government built homes on the prairie. There was even a scheme to bring over a hundred schoolboys to learn to become farmers.

The government and the railway also used publicity to encourage immigration. They produced brochures, posters, newspaper ads, displays —

even motion pictures. These publicity materials showed pictures of vast sunlit plains covered in lush golden crops and populated by rosy-cheeked families. One young Londoner remembers a poster showing a field full of waving dollar bills.

Children's magazines contributed to this romantic portrait of Canada. In stories and pictures Canada was portrayed as a land of outdoor adventure — galloping across the prairie, hunting, fishing, encounters with coyotes and grizzlies, a do-it-yourself world of freedom and challenge. To someone from a noisy, crowded city like London, where the only open place to play was the cemetery, it must have looked like heaven.

The problem with this picture of Canada is that it was an exaggeration. One immigrant woman described the "cottage" that she had been promised: "A hen house no windows half a door no stove or bed nothing but hen feed." Much of the best farmland had already been assigned and some of the settlers ended up in a desert-like region of the prairies called the prairie dry belt, an area where special farming techniques are required.

The promotional literature for immigrants also underplayed the harsh climate of the prairies. The *Canadian Settler's Handbook* assured potential immigrants that the climate was "healthful" and that "brilliant sunshine produces a sense of invigoration." It neglected to mention storms so severe that cattle froze to death. Another exaggeration involved the warm reception immigrants were led to expect. In fact, Canadians were not universally welcoming to the English, whom many regarded as arrogant and snobbish. Finally, the jobs that the government promised did not always exist. One angry immigrant wrote, in 1929, that it was "all lies they [tell] you up at Canada House London."

Many prairie immigrants of this period just didn't make it. Of the 3,000 families in the 3,000 Scheme, 2,000 ended up leaving the region. Some families went to the cities of eastern Canada, where there were more jobs. Some men went to construction camps in the north. Some went south to the United States. Some gave up and returned to England.

For selected newcomers the immigrant dream came true. Blessed with a magic combination of hard work, initiative, support and good luck they flourished on the prairies. But many more simply made the best of it, pinning their immigrant hopes on the next generation. They raised children who came to regard Canada as home, and they in turn raised children who had never known another homeland.

When we look around a classroom of today we see, among the faces, some who are descendants of those English immigrants, strong people who took the huge risk of planting themselves in a new home.

Advertisements such as this Canada West poster promised immigrants a better life once they settled in the west.

Family photo on board the Ausonia.

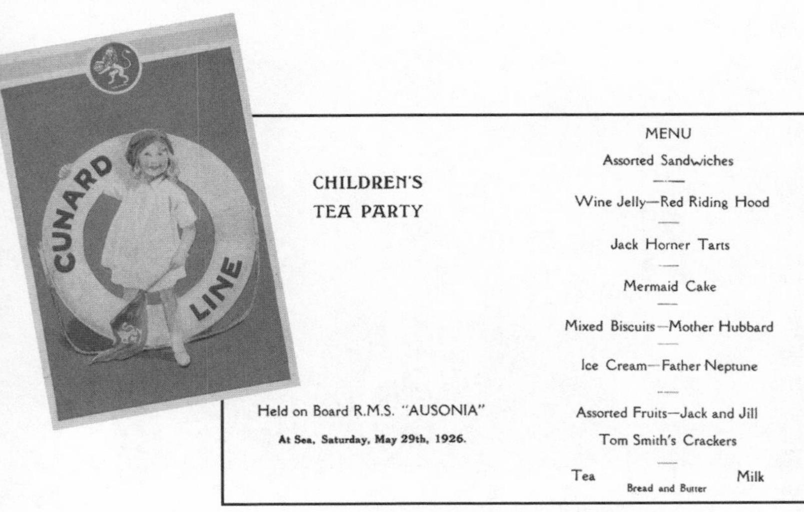

CHILDREN'S
TEA PARTY

Held on Board R.M.S. "AUSONIA"

At Sea, Saturday, May 29th, 1926.

MENU

Assorted Sandwiches

Wine Jelly—Red Riding Hood

Jack Horner Tarts

Mermaid Cake

Mixed Biscuits—Mother Hubbard

Ice Cream—Father Neptune

Assorted Fruits—Jack and Jill

Tom Smith's Crackers

Tea Milk

Bread and Butter

Invitation to children's tea party aboard the Ausonia.

A poster encouraging immigrants to come to the Canadian west to "build your nest."

The prairie stretches far out behind these children from the Lloydminster area.

The Moaner children on horseback, Milo area of Alberta, in the 1920s.

Students outside a typical one-room prairie school — Reid Hill School in Vulcan, Alberta, 1921.

This class photo from Spring Coulee School in 1924 shows a typical prairie classroom.

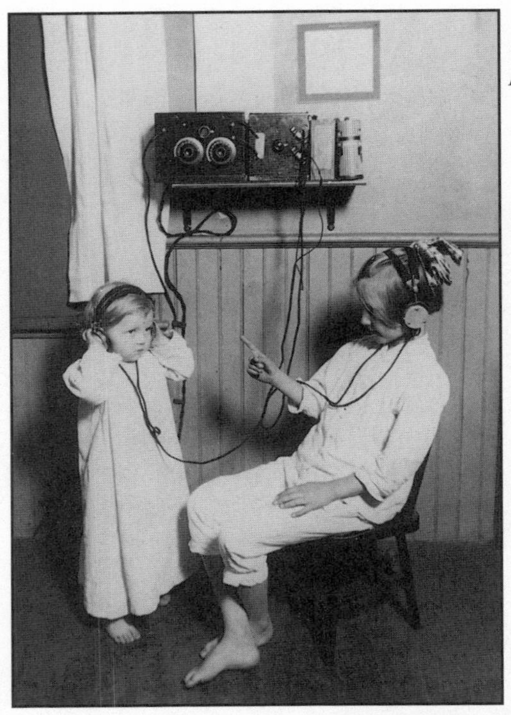

Children using earphones to listen to their favourite programs on the radio.

Making ice cream by hand in 1926. The ice cream mixture in the centre metal container is cooled by the surrounding ice and salt.

Ladies' nail-hammering contest at a picnic in Box Springs, Alberta, in the 1920s.

Stooking wheat by hand in Saskatchewan in 1928.

The grain elevator at Norquay, Saskatchewan, June, 1920.

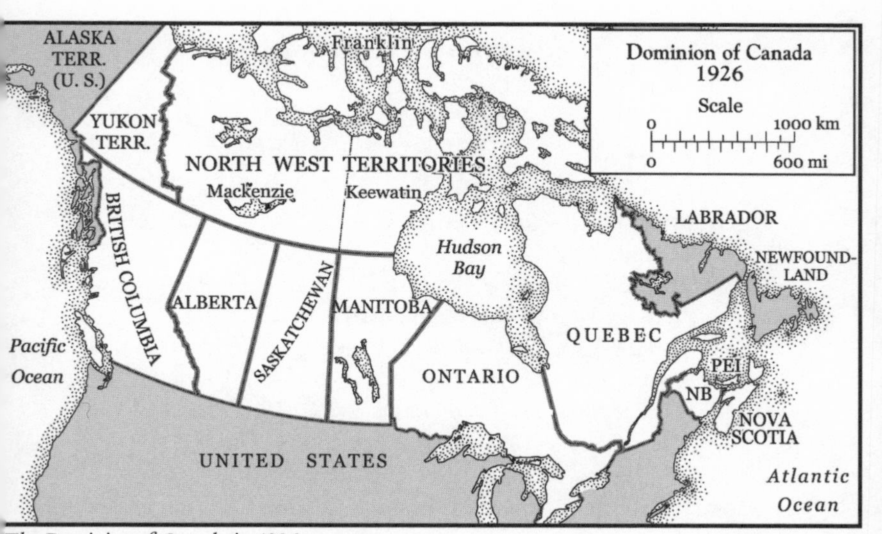

The Dominion of Canada in 1926.

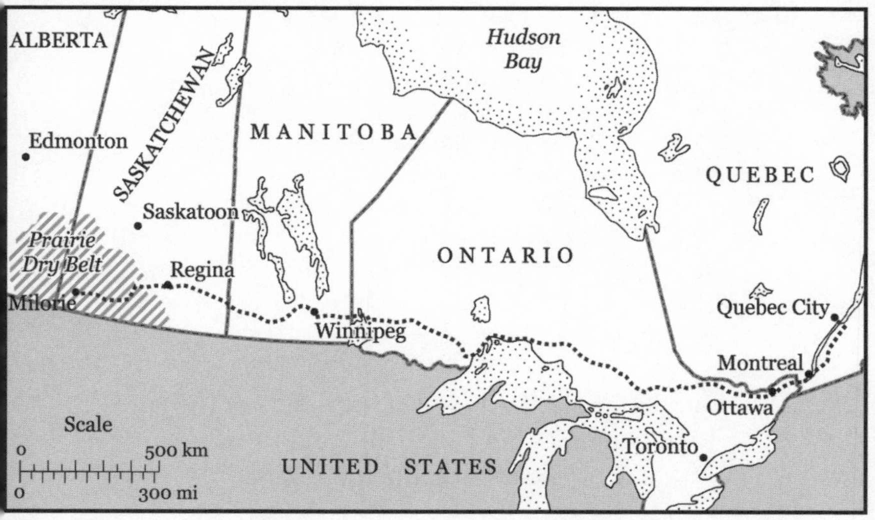

The Weatheralls' route to Milorie, showing their disembarkation point in Quebec City, and their train route across the country to the Prairie Dry Belt area in southwestern Saskatchewan.

Acknowledgments

Grateful acknowledgment is made for permission to reprint the following:
Cover portrait: Glenbow Archives, Calgary, Canada, detail from Sheffield Family photo, colourized (NA-105-5).
Cover background: Her Majesty the Queen in Right of Canada as represented by the Canadian Tourism Commission.
Page 193: Glenbow Archives Pam 971.2 C212 c 1925.
Page 194: Author's collection.
Page 195: National Archives of Canada C126302.
Page 196 upper: National Archives of Canada C30784.
Page 196 lower: Glenbow Archives NA-1367-90.
Page 197 upper: Glenbow Archives NA-2416-4.
Page 197 lower: Glenbow Archives NA-2894-6.
Page 198 upper: City of Toronto Archives SC 244, Item 8054.
Page 198 lower: Glenbow Archives NA-2506-6.
Page 199 upper: Glenbow Archives NA-2927-13.
Page 199 lower: National Archives of Canada C7786.
Page 200: Saskatchewan Archives Board SAB R-A2260(2).
Page 201: Maps by Paul Heersink/Paperglyphs. Map data © 2000 Government of Canada with permission from Natural Resources Canada.

Thanks to Barbara Hehner for her checking of the manuscript, and Dr. Bill Waiser for sharing his historical expertise.

In memory of my mother,
Ruth Elizabeth Steabner Ellis

With thanks to those who told me their stories:
May Ellis, Link Steabner, Thelma Drinnan,
William Lawrence, Margaret Bykevich and,
most of all, my dad, Joseph Ellis.

About the Author

A Prairie as Wide as the Sea is Sarah Ellis's tenth book for young readers. She has won many awards, among them the Governor General's Award for *Pick-Up Sticks,* Mr. Christie's Book Award for *Out of the Blue* and the Sheila A. Egoff Children's Book Prize for *The Baby Project.* In 1995 Sarah was honoured with the Vicky Metcalf Award for her body of work.

"When I was a kid," she says, "my favourite told stories were my parents' stories of the 'olden days.' These were of two kinds — Dad's stories of growing up in east London and Mum's of small-town Saskatchewan. . . . Many of these stories, moulded to fit my own, made their way into *A Prairie as Wide as the Sea*."

While researching this book, Sarah was going through 1920s microfilm files for what was then called the *Regina Leader*. Its Saturday supplement, called the Torchbearer's Club, contained news about kids' daily lives, everything from chasing gophers to tipping over outhouses. Even though the microfilm print was tiny, Sarah kept reading, looking for information about April Fools' Day. "Would somebody have written an account of the tricks they played in school and at home?" Sarah said. "I whirred my last reel over to the relevant Saturday of 1927, just on the off chance. The headline to one letter, Childhood Pranks, seemed promising. I started to read, squinting and straining over the blotchy screen, and then I glanced down at the signature. Right there, in a library that is so new that it still smells like carpets, in the cold grey light of an uncongenial technology, I was visited by a ghost. The author of the letter was my mother, aged thirteen. She stood in front of me, present, substantial, immediate . . . " Sarah's mother had died decades earlier, so finding this letter from her mother, then a girl herself, was "a gift" — something Sarah had never expected to uncover while doing research about the character she would come to call Ivy.

"On first reading, the letter revealed a person I never knew. She was cheeky, a bit of a cut-up. Where was my quiet, contained, middle-aged mother? On a second reading, however, I met a person I knew well. My mother grew up with affectionate brothers. So did I. She liked slang. So do I. She enjoyed stories about herself as a little kid, as told by her mother. So did I. Most of all, she was obviously a writer. Me too. It is even harder to read microfilm when you're crying."

In addition to her own writing, Sarah reviews children's literature for journals such as *Quill & Quire* and *The Hornbook*. She is a librarian and a member of IBBY, the Vancouver Children's Literature Round Table, The Vancouver Storytelling Circle, the Writer's Union, PEN and CANSCAIP.

While the events described and some of the characters in this book may be based on actual historical events and real people, Ivy Doris Weatherall is a fictional character, created by the author, and her diary and its epilogue are works of fiction.

Copyright © 2001 by Sarah Ellis.

All rights reserved. Published by Scholastic Canada Ltd.
SCHOLASTIC and DEAR CANADA and logos are trademarks and/or registered trademarks of Scholastic Inc.

National Library of Canada Cataloguing in Publication Data

Ellis, Sarah
A prairie as wide as the sea : the immigrant diary of Ivy Weatherall

(Dear Canada)
ISBN 0-439-98833-0

1. British – Saskatchewan – Juvenile fiction. I. Title. II. Series.

PS8559.L57P72 2001 jC813'.54 C2001-930336-X
PZ7.E4758Pr 2001

No part of this publication may be reproduced or stored in a retrieval system, or transmitted in any form or by any means, electronic, mechanical, recording, or otherwise, without written permission of the publisher, Scholastic Canada Ltd., 175 Hillmount Road, Markham, Ontario, Canada L6C 1Z7. In the case of photocopying or other reprographic copying, a licence must be obtained from CANCOPY (Canadian Copyright Licensing Agency), 1 Yonge Street East, Suite 1900, Toronto, Ontario, M5E 1E5.
5 4 3 2 1 Printed in Canada 1 2 3 4 5/0

The display type was set in Tiffany Bold Italic.
The text type was set in Tiffany Light.

Printed in Canada
First printing, September 2001